THE PLAYBOY OF HARLEY STREET

BY
ANNE FRASER

MILLS & BOON

Falkirk Council		
GM		
Askews & Holts		
AF		£13.99

First published in Great Britain 2011
by Mills & Boon, an imprint of Harlequin (UK) Limited.
Large Print edition 2012
Harlequin (UK) Limited, Eton House,
18-24 Paradise Road, Richmond, Surrey TW9 1SR

© Anne Fraser 2011

ISBN: 978 0 263 22422 1

Printed and bound in Great Britain
by CPI Antony Rowe, Chippenham, Wiltshire

Anne Fraser was born in Scotland, but brought up in South Africa. After she left school she returned to the birthplace of her parents, the remote Western Islands of Scotland. She left there to train as a nurse, before going on to university to study English Literature. After the birth of her first child she and her doctor husband travelled the world, working in rural Africa, Australia and Northern Canada. Anne still works in the health sector. To relax, she enjoys spending time with her family, reading, walking and travelling.

Recent titles by the same author:

THE DOCTOR AND THE DEBUTANTE
DAREDEVIL, DOCTOR…DAD!†
PRINCE CHARMING OF HARLEY STREET
RESCUED: MOTHER AND BABY
MIRACLE: MARRIAGE REUNITED
SPANISH DOCTOR, PREGNANT MIDWIFE*

The Brides of Penhally Bay
†*St Piran's Hospital*

These books are also available in eBook format from www.millsandboon.co.uk

CHAPTER ONE

KATIE SIMPSON looked around the luxury interior of the private jet and wanted to pinch herself. Dr Cavendish, the senior partner at the practice, had told her at her interview that she'd be expected to fly all over the world, but he hadn't said anything about private jets.

Katie jiggled her legs impatiently. Where was Dr Lineham? They had boarded the small plane ten minutes ago and there was no sign of her colleague. Opposite her, their patient was playing a game on her games console, looking completely unfazed by her surroundings.

Lucy Hargreaves was eight years old and suffering from cystic fibrosis. Katie and Dr Lineham were accompanying her to Monaco so that she could watch her father, a British racing champion, in a prestigious racing tournament.

Katie swivelled round in her seat at the sound of footsteps clattering up the aluminium steps.

Dr Lineham at last—and not before time. For the second time that day, Katie was taken aback. Instead of the older man she'd envisaged, Dr Lineham was lean, with thick, tousled dark hair that curled over his collar, olive skin, high cheekbones and a wide, full mouth. His tall, broad-shouldered frame filled the doorway as he paused to finish adjusting his tie and do up the top button of his shirt. He looked more like a film star than a doctor.

'Damn London traffic,' he muttered, before coming forward. He stopped next to Lucy and ruffled her hair. 'Hi, Luce. You okay?'

Lucy glanced up, her eyes crinkled in a smile. 'Hey, Dr Fabio. Where've you been? Late night out again?'

Fabio held a finger to his lips and pretended to frown. 'Luce, don't give away my secrets. For all you know, I've been in the hospital all night.'

He winked at the little girl and she giggled.

Oh, please, Katie thought. Couldn't he at least pretend to be more professional?

Deep green eyes swept over Katie. She was aware of him taking in her dark suit and sensible shoes and shifted uncomfortably under his appraising look. She hadn't known what to wear so had settled on the same outfit she had worn to her interview. Not that Dr Lineham had been there. Apparently he'd been away with a patient in Mauritius or some other exotic island.

'And is this our new physio, Lucy?' His voice was as smooth as warm chocolate with just a trace of an accent Katie didn't recognise.

'She says I can call her Katie,' Lucy replied. 'She's been here for ages already. She knows how to play games on my console. I think she's cool.'

'I'm pleased to meet you, Dr Lineham,' Katie responded, trying to keep the disapproval from her voice. Despite being told at her interview that the practice was friendly and informal, it had been emphasised that all the staff took their duty towards their patients seriously. Katie expected nothing less, but now she wondered if one of her colleagues didn't share that ethos. Imagine coming directly to work after being out all night! What was he thinking? He should have left home earlier if he didn't want to be late. Like she had. An hour and a half before she'd had to, and if it had meant she'd had to hang around the airport for quite a while, at least she'd been on time.

And didn't Dr Lineham need to check Lucy over or something? Katie was far from reassured by his casual approach. Between them, they had total responsibility for their patient.

Dr Lineham held out his hand and as Katie shook it, she was aware of the hardness of his skin, which didn't quite fit with his groomed exterior. 'And I am pleased to meet you too, Katie Simpson, but, please, call me Fabio.'

The way he said her name in an accent she still couldn't quite place sent an unexpected frisson up her spine.

'You have to strap yourself in,' Lucy reminded Katie, as Fabio settled himself into the seat opposite. 'Just for take-off.'

Lucy was pale and underweight for her age but with a wisdom in her indigo-coloured eyes that belied her years. Dr Cavendish, the senior partner, had briefed Katie the day before about the little girl's condition.

'Her CF is under control most of the time, but unfortunately she has had one or two bad chest infections and there is some scarring.'

'Should she be travelling?' Katie had asked.

'It makes her happy. And after all the trip is

only for two days and as long as she gets regular physio and Fabio is there with her, there's no reason to think she won't be absolutely fine. Our clinic is set up so that we can allow our patients to carry on with their normal lives as much as possible.

'For those patients that can manage it, naturally we see them at the practice, otherwise we attend them in their own homes or wherever they may be. Sometimes a patient may need us to travel with them and we do that too. We aim to be as flexible as possible.

'Mrs Hargreaves—Amelia—wouldn't be letting Lucy go if she didn't have medical support for her and absolute faith in us,' Dr Cavendish continued. 'Dr Lineham has been looking after Lucy for the last two years—a year before he joined us—and her parents have complete and justified confidence in him.' He smiled. 'Lucy has never seen her father race—at least, not apart from on television—so she's adamant she wants to go. As you'll learn, she's quite a determined child.'

As the plane gathered speed for take-off, Katie gripped the armrests of her seat. Fabio, on the other hand, was casually flicking through a magazine as if he didn't have a care in the world. His legs were stretched out in front of him and Katie couldn't help but notice how the material of his suit trousers clung to his thighs, emphasising the defined muscles. He had loosened his tie and discarded his jacket and looked very much at home. Something about him sent a shiver of disquiet through her.

'Don't be scared,' Lucy said, placing one of her small hands on top of Katie's.

Not good. The child comforting the adult. Katie forced herself to unpick the fingers of her right hand from the armrests and relax.

'I'll be fine. Keep it between you and me, Lucy, but I've never flown in a plane this size before. It doesn't even feel like a plane. I guess it just takes getting used to.'

Lucy had given her a quick tour before they'd prepared for take-off. There were twelve seats in groups of four with a table between them, a bar with fruit juice and snacks, and shelves with books and magazines. It reminded her more of a lobby of a hotel than a plane. The co-pilot, a slim, attractive woman who looked far too young to be flying planes, doubled up as the stewardess and had introduced herself simply as Fern.

As soon as they were airborne and the seat-belt lights switched off, Lucy put down her games console and showed Katie how one of the seats at the rear of the cabin could be made into a bed. 'That way I can lie down while you do my physio.'

'Have you been to Monaco before?' Lucy asked, as Katie worked on her.

Katie smiled. 'I've spent three weeks in Europe and I've just returned from working in Ireland, but that's about the limit of my travels, I'm afraid.'

'I haven't been to Monaco either. But I have stayed on the yacht we're staying on before when we've been on holiday. I like staying on yachts. Do you?'

'I did a trip on a riverboat with my parents when I was a little girl. It was wonderful. I loved it. It was so much fun. I remember my brother and I had to keep getting on and off to open the locks.'

At the memory, a stab of pain shot through her and her eyes filled. She was glad Lucy was lying on her stomach and wouldn't see the tears threatening to spill. Would she ever be able to think of Richard without wanting to howl? She doubted it. She breathed deeply, trying to keep her voice level.

'Okay, that's you.' Katie helped Lucy sit up.

'That was quick,' Lucy said. 'You're much better than the person who normally does my physio.'

Kate smiled. 'Maybe because I've had lots of practice. My young cousin has cystic fibrosis too. I used to do her physio when they lived near me.'

'Want another shot at my game?' Lucy asked when they were seated again. 'I don't mind sharing.'

She really was an extremely likeable little girl. 'No, thanks, sweetheart, but it's kind of you to offer. I think I'll read for a little while.'

Katie tried to concentrate on the magazine she'd bought in Departures, but somehow her eyes kept on straying over towards her colleague as he chatted to Lucy. Dr Fabio Lineham was the most extraordinarily gorgeous man she'd ever set eyes on. And she bet he knew it too. No doubt he had a phone full of women's phone numbers. She started guiltily when he caught her flicking a glance at him and she made a show of being deeply engrossed in reading an article. Until she noticed the title—'How to Entice Your Man into Your Heart and Between the Sheets'. She slapped the pages shut when Fabio left Lucy playing her game and sat down beside her.

'So, Katie, I think we should get to know each other, seeing as we'll be working together.'

He smelled divine. A mixture of spice and lemons. Her heart gave a little run of beats and for some reason she felt the air had been sucked from the atmosphere, leaving her feeling breath-less.

'What would you like to know?' Katie asked, relieved that her voice didn't give her odd reaction away.

'Everything.' He glanced at his watch. 'We've a couple of hours to go yet.'

'There's not much to tell, really.' At least, there wasn't much she *wanted* to tell him. She liked to keep her professional and personal lives separate.

'I've been working as a physio for four years. I specialised in sports injuries before moving to paediatrics.' There. Keep it to work. That was safe ground.

'I know that. It was all on your pretty impressive CV. By the way, well done on that paper you contributed to the *British Medical Journal*.'

The paper wasn't listed on her CV and she was surprised he knew about it.

'I enjoyed reading about bioethics and physiotherapy. It's not something I knew much about.'

So, he hadn't just glanced at it but read it. She looked at him more closely. Perhaps she shouldn't make up her mind so quickly? Didn't she hate it when other people did that? Just because he was good looking—strike that, amazing looking—it didn't mean he wasn't a good doctor. She relaxed a little.

'I'd like to know about you,' he added. 'Not just your professional résumé.'

She stiffened. Perhaps she should trust her instincts after all? She was right about one thing. He was the kind of man who couldn't bear to pass up a chance to flirt with anyone of the opposite sex. He was gorgeous and knew it. She distrusted men like that. Not that she had any experience of his kind of man.

'Not much to tell, really,' she said.

'Ah, I'm sure there is. What do you like to do in your spare time?'

Katie looked at him out of the corner of her eye. 'I exercise when I can. Swimming mostly. And I go out occasionally.'

'No boyfriend?'

It was none of his business. This was taking polite interest a step too far.

'No,' she replied shortly. 'Tell me about you.' It was a safe ploy. Men like him liked nothing better than to talk about themselves.

To her surprise, he shook his head. 'Oh, no, you don't. I asked first.' He smiled and her pulse did another little run of beats. 'Tell me about the swimming. Do you go often? What else do you do to keep fit?'

The approval as his dark green eyes swept across her body brought a flush to her cheeks. Really, if she hadn't just met him, and he wasn't her boss, she'd be tempted to… What? Tell him to stop looking at her? It wasn't necessarily his fault her body was behaving in this disconcerting, alien manner.

'I swim almost every day. It's a habit I got into as a child and have somehow managed to keep up. I find it relaxing. Nothing to do except think about finishing the lengths. No noise. Just mindless rhythm.' At least, that was how it used to be. These days any silence was filled with memories of Richard and terrible, overwhelming pain, loss and guilt. No matter how hard she pushed herself, no matter how many times she pounded up and down the length of the pool, she could never exhaust herself enough to sleep without having stomach-churning, terrifying nightmares.

She forced herself to concentrate on the present. 'What about you?' This was more like it. Two colleagues exchanging polite small talk. 'I take it you're into the party scene?' She couldn't resist it.

Fabio leant over, his warm breath fanning her neck. It took every ounce of her willpower not to instinctively pull away from him as sparks danced down her spine. 'Don't tell Lucy—she likes to think I lead an exciting life of parties and balls, but...' he dropped his voice to a conspiratorial whisper '...actually, I had to attend a formal dinner last night but was called out in the middle of it to attend to a patient. I had to admit her to hospital and we were there most of the night. I didn't have time to go home and change.'

'Oh.' So she had got him all wrong. She felt a tell-tale flush colour her cheeks.

He resumed his normal tone. 'But to answer your initial question, I love all sports.'

'He goes BASE jumping,' Lucy interjected from across the way. She'd obviously been listening to their conversation while playing her game. 'It's how he met my dad. Dad used to do it too but Mum made him give it up. She said it was too dangerous and that it was bad enough him being a racing driver without that as well.'

What could be more dangerous than driving a racing car?

'What's BASE jumping?' Katie asked. 'I can't say I've ever heard of it.'

'It stands for Buildings Antenna Spans and Earth. I looked it up in a book,' Lucy replied.

Katie was none the wiser.

'Earth actually stands for cliffs,' Fabio said. 'You find a cliff with sheer sides and jump off it.'

'You jump off cliffs?' Katie couldn't keep the incredulity from her voice.

Fabio shrugged. 'It's not as dangerous as it sounds. I do wear a parachute.'

'I couldn't imagine in my wildest dreams throwing myself off a mountain with nothing but a flimsy bit of material strapped to my back.' Katie shivered. 'Bit of an extreme way to get a high, isn't it?'

'Some people get their thrills from a bottle. I guess I get mine at the top of a mountain.'

It was the way he said it that made Katie look more closely at him. There was a far-away look in his eyes, a sudden seriousness that intrigued her. Suddenly she wanted to know what attracted him to such a dangerous sport.

Fabio seemed to give himself a mental shake.

'But we were talking about you. Where do you live? And what about your family? Are they nearby?'

Katie swallowed. 'I stay in North London, not far from where I was brought up. Dad was an accountant. Mum used to work as a nurse in the local hospital.'

'Used to?' Fabio looked at her sharply.

Oh, God, she always dreaded this question. It made people embarrassingly uncomfortable and they usually quickly moved the conversation to safer ground. Not that she could blame them—what was there to say? 'They died in a plane crash when I was thirteen.'

There was no disguising the shock and genuine sympathy in his dark green eyes. 'I am so sorry. That must have been hard, losing both of them.' Fabio touched her hand lightly.

'It was.' Her heart thumped against her chest. She guessed what was coming next.

'What about brothers? Sisters?'

Katie flinched and shook her head. He'd already elicited much more information than she was comfortable with—and what could she say to this virtual stranger about her brother? Especially when she was still so raw she could barely acknowledge the truth herself?

'No. It's just me.' Even as she said it, she hated that she couldn't yet bring herself to mention her brother. But she couldn't. Not without wanting to cry.

She needed to turn the conversation back to safe ground. Anywhere but on her family life. Forcing a smile, Katie turned to him. 'And you? Where are you from? Not England, I'm guessing.'

'So where do you think, then?' he asked with a crooked smile.

She leaned her head back and made a show of thinking. 'Portugal.'

Fabio wiggled his hand in a side-to-side gesture. 'Hmm, not quite. Brazil.'

Brazeel. The way he said it made it sound so exotic.

'That's a long way from your family.'

'My mother lives in Brazil most of the time, it's where most of her work is. My father died when I was in my teens.'

'I'm sorry,' Kate said simply.

'His mother is a film star,' Lucy piped up again. The child had remarkable hearing.

'Hey, don't you give all my secrets away, Luce,' Fabio protested.

Katie sneaked a sideways look at Fabio. It made sense he'd have an actress as a mother. That was probably where he got his stunning good looks. She raised an eyebrow, inviting him to elaborate.

'You might have heard of her. The actress Camilla Salvatore?' The way he said his mother's name, rolling the consonants around his tongue, his Brazilian accent becoming stronger, made

Katie's toes curl, even as she wondered what had caused the bleak look in his eyes.

Camilla Salvatore—who hadn't heard of her? If Katie remembered rightly, she had been a model before becoming an actress, the wife of the equally famous Tom Lineham, who had been huge in the 1980s and whose hits were still popular even now.

Tom Lineham! God. That made Fabio his son.

Fabio must have read the dawning realisation in her face. 'Yes. 'Fraid so. They're my folks.'

Katie's head was spinning. The couple had been international celebrities. She remembered reading somewhere that Tom Lineham had died and that there had been some mystery surrounding the circumstances, but wasn't that always the case with celebrities? It was hardly something she could quiz his son about. It wasn't surprising she hadn't made the connection, between Dr Fabio Lineham and Tom Lineham. It had never crossed her mind that two famous people would have a son who had become a doctor. Why had he anyway? It seemed an unusual choice for the child of extremely wealthy parents.

'Yet you became a doctor,' she said.

He looked amused. 'As opposed to what? Being in the movies? A singer? Lolling about, living off my parents' money?' He smiled wryly. No doubt he was used to this reaction. 'I'm a lousy actor and my voice is worse.'

'So all this…' she waved a hand around the interior of the plane '…is pretty much old hat to you.'

''Fraid so,' he said again. 'I didn't even know there were commercial aircraft until I was thirteen or so.'

Poor little rich boy.

A flicker of a smile crossed his face. 'That didn't come out too well, did it? But I'm not going to apologise for the way I was brought up. There was money, yes. But as for…' He stopped suddenly but not before Katie thought a flash of pain in his eyes. Almost immediately it was gone and the mask was back in place. 'One thing I've learned, Katie Simpson. Never apologise for who you are. Or what you were. Never look back. It's the here and now that matters.'

What did he mean by that? For a second she wondered if he knew about Richard. But that was impossible. She hadn't told anyone. She was beginning to get the unsettling sensation he could see inside her head.

'And, before you ask, no brothers, no sisters—only a cousin who lives in California.' Maybe he *could* read her mind.

'So what made you choose physiotherapy?' Fabio said, before she could question him further.

'My young cousin has CF. Like all sufferers, she has to get physio regularly. She's one of the lucky ones, though.'

Her cousin had escaped the relentless round of chest infections that most CF patients were susceptible to throughout their lives.

'What about you? Why did you become a doctor?' Katie tried to turn the conversation back to him. She was reluctant to share any more details of her life with this man. He already knew more about her than she wanted him to know.

'Pretty much the same reason as you—personal experience. I was ill as a child—nothing too serious. I found it really interesting what everyone was doing around me and decided I'd like to be on the right end of a needle.' His words trailed off and Katie thought something shifted in his eyes before his mouth widened in a smile. 'Seems

we have more in common than just being colleagues.'

Katie was pretty sure they didn't have much in
common. Apart from the fact they had both lost
their fathers, his upbringing couldn't have been
more different from hers. He was rich, sophisticated and probably used to socialising with the
kind of people she'd only read about. Further-
more, the way he looked, the confidence that
seemed to ooze from every pore, made her feel
gauche and unsophisticated. He had no right to
make her feel like that.

'I doubt that.' As soon as the words were out of
her mouth she realised how abrupt she sounded.
'I'm sorry, that didn't come out the way I intended.'

'That's okay,' He gave her a puzzled look. He
was probably wondering why she was so prickly.
She wasn't sure herself. Ever since he'd stepped
on board, she'd felt flustered.

She picked up her magazine again, making it
obvious she preferred to read than chat.

Fabio gave her a long look before settling himself back in his seat and closing his eyes. He
opened one briefly to look at Katie. 'Give me a

nudge when we're about to land, would you? It was a hell of a late night last night.'

Before Katie could reply, the rhythm of his breathing changed and within seconds he was sound asleep.

CHAPTER TWO

As soon as the plane touched down, the co-pilot returned to open the door and release the stairs. As they left the plane, Katie saw the statuesque blonde slip a piece of paper to Fabio. Her contact details, no doubt.

Lucy let out a squeal of delight and almost ran down the steep steps towards a slim, elegant woman and a stocky man, who had to be her parents from the delighted expressions on their faces.

Lucy's father swung her into his arms and held her tight, whilst her mother smothered her with kisses.

Katie hesitated at the bottom of the stairs, reluctant to intrude. Tears clogged her throat as she watched their emotional family reunion, suddenly stricken by a sense of loneliness and longing.

But she couldn't let her personal feelings over-whelm her—she was here to do a job—and perform it professionally. Forcing herself to breathe slowly and evenly, Katie regained her composure. Besides, what would it be like to have a child not knowing how long she'd be with you? Unbearable. As bad as having a son or brother or any loved one in a war zone. Life had taught her one thing. Happiness wasn't guaranteed and even this couple, for all their fame and fortune, weren't immune to the roll of the dice. Katie prayed Lucy's parents would have their daughter for a long, long time to come.

'Fabio.' Amelia walked towards them, hand held outstretched. She seemed pleased, even relieved to see him. He bent to let her kiss him on both cheeks. 'How lovely to see you again,' Amelia said. 'We can't thank you enough for coming.'

Amelia looked elegantly cool in a vanilla-white trouser suit with just the merest pink lace of her camisole peeking out. She was made up but no amount of make-up could hide the fear and sadness in her eyes. She turned to Katie and held out her hand. 'Miss Simpson, I can't tell you how delighted I am that you could come too. Lucy has been dy...' she bit her lip '...longing to see her daddy race, but we couldn't bring her. Until now. I'm told that you are an expert in the field of physio for CF.'

'I'm happy to be here too, Mrs Hargreaves. I gave Lucy her physio on the plane. Didn't I, Luce?'

'Please, do call me Amelia.' She knelt beside her daughter. 'Did you sleep on the plane, sweet pea?'

'Yes. A little.'

'Hey, Fabio!' Mark called out. 'Great to see you again.'

Katie watched as the two men greeted each other warmly, hugging and slapping each other on the back. Fabio clearly had a stronger relationship with the family than most doctors did with patients and their families.

After introductions all round, Mark gathered Lucy up into his arms again. 'Sorry I have to leave you straight away, sweetie, but there's a team meeting I have to attend.' Giving his wife a lingering kiss, Mark sketched a wave and jumped into a low-slung sports car, then roared away.

'I'll take you to the yacht,' Amelia said. 'The firm my husband races for has given us sole use of it for however long we need, whenever we need it. There's plenty of room. I hope you'll be comfortable.'

They all piled into the back of a stretch limo. The limo was another first for Katie and she sank back in the leather seat.

As Lucy chatted away to her mother, Katie stared out of the darkened rear windows of the car. She had heard about Monaco. With its international reputation for being the playground of the rich and famous, who hadn't?

It was like being on a film set. Sleek sports cars purred around. She didn't know the names of most of them, but they could have come straight out of a James Bond movie. Most of them were open to the sunshine and were driven by men and women who looked as if they'd just stepped out of the pages of a glossy magazine or starred in that same movie.

Fabio found himself tuning out from Lucy's excited chatter, watching Katie instead. Every now and again, her eyes would light up and then just as quickly she would bite her lip and look anxious. It was extraordinary—and curiously refreshing—to see every reaction reflected in her face. Most women he knew thought it gauche to show emotion, especially to reveal that they were anything but bored by their surroundings. Katie Simpson intrigued him.

Not that she was his cup of tea. She was prim and serious in her buttoned-up suit, and there was that disconcerting shadow in her eyes. He liked his women sophisticated and, well, to put it frankly, not too deep.

And there were definitely deep layers to Katie Simpson. He had yet to meet someone who didn't enjoy talking about themselves but it was obvious that she was the exception to the rule. There were times on the plane when he could have sworn she was hiding something. Back there on the tarmac, he'd seen sadness wash over her face as she'd witnessed the Hargreaves' reunion. Was she recovering from a broken heart? A jilted lover, perhaps? It was a possibility. So that sealed it. Even if she had been his type, he would never have an affair with a vulnerable woman who was on the rebound. That was a complication he could do without. And he didn't do complicated.

* * *

Despite the evidence of wealth everywhere, nothing could have prepared Katie for the actual size of the yacht.

Moored alongside several others, it wasn't the biggest in the bay, but it was still larger than anything Katie had ever seen. More like a small cruise ship than a pleasure boat.

'I'll show you to your cabins,' Amelia said as she led them up the gangway. 'Then, if you think Lucy's up to it, I promised I'd take her to the track. Mark is due to start a practice session in an hour.' Her anxious eyes found Fabio's. 'If you think it would be okay for Lucy to be there? You will come too, won't you?'

Fabio touched her on the shoulder. 'Lucy's doing really well at the moment and of course we'll come to the track. That's what we're here for.'

'You're such a worry-wart, Mummy,' Lucy said. 'I keep telling you I'm okay. There's no way I'm not going to watch Daddy.' The little girl's mouth was set in a firm line. This was the determined side to Lucy Dr Cavendish had told her about. Determination was good.

'I guess all mothers and fathers worry about

their children,' Amelia said lightly. 'Even when they're all grown up. It's part of loving someone very much.'

It was true, Katie thought, her heart twisting. Unfortunately all the worrying in the world didn't stop bad things from happening.

Amelia hooked her arm through Fabio's, leaving Katie to follow in their wake. To her surprise she felt a small hand slip into hers. She looked down to find Lucy looking up at her.

'Don't be sad,' she said. 'I'll look after you.'

Katie squeezed Lucy's hand. No doubt the little girl was used to seeing the hurt in adults' eyes. Katie gave herself a mental shake and forced a smile. For as long as she was there, she would make certain Lucy had one less adult to worry about.

'Sure,' Katie replied. She dropped her voice and bent to whisper in the little girl's ear. 'This is a bit bigger than the boat I was on as a little girl, you know.'

Lucy giggled. 'It's not that big, silly.' She pulled on Katie's arm. 'Come and see.'

It *was* that big. There was a hot tub surrounded by padded seating and a raised deck for sunbathing. To the stern was a covered area where, Lucy explained, they had breakfast. A number of white-uniformed staff drifted around with trays of cool drinks and Katie helped herself to a glass of chilled freshly squeezed orange juice. It was the perfect cure for her tight, aching throat.

After showing her the top deck, Lucy led her down some steps.

The inside was even more spectacular. An enormous lounge with what looked like a working fireplace was furnished with soft white leather couches and antique pieces, including a polished rosewood table that held a silver decanter and crystal goblets. The dining room was equally impressive. A chandelier hung over a French-polished dining table with matching chairs. It was big enough to seat sixteen. Katie hardly had time to take it all in as Lucy kept pulling her along until they came to a door. Lucy opened it with a flourish.

'This is your cabin. Dr Fabio's is right next door. And mine is across the passage, next to Mummy and Daddy's.'

Cabin wasn't the word Katie would have used to describe the room. There was a double bed, a sitting area with a television and a marble bath-room with a full bath and shower. Katie, with Lucy still watching her reaction, stepped out onto a small balcony. The marina was crammed full of yachts, most of which had people on the decks either sunbathing or sipping drinks while they chatted. Katie couldn't be sure, but she thought she recognised at least one famous actor.

'Wow!' she said to Lucy. She couldn't think of anything else to say.

Suddenly the little girl seemed exhausted and she sank back on Katie's bed. Katie was instantly alarmed. The long journey plus the excitement had taken it out of the child.

'Tell you what,' she said. 'While I unpack, why don't you have a nap on my bed before it's time to go to the race track? Then, if you don't feel better, I'll ask Dr Lineham to come and have a listen to your chest.'

'I'm okay,' Lucy said. 'But I will have a sleep. Don't say anything to Mum, will you? She's happy right now.'

Katie's heart went out to Lucy. Along the way she had become used to pretending for her mother's sake.

Lucy was asleep in seconds and Katie was covering her with a blanket when there was a knock on the door. She answered it and put her finger to her lips when she saw Fabio standing there. He'd changed out of his suit and into a pair of light trousers and an open-necked, short-sleeved shirt. Katie felt over dressed in her jacket and trousers.

He glanced over her shoulder and, seeing Lucy, tiptoed into the room. 'I was just looking for her,' he whispered. 'How's she doing?'

'Exhausted, I think. I suggested she have her nap here, where I can keep an eye on her. I think it's all been too much for her. The journey, the excitement of seeing her parents, as well as the prospect of watching her father race.'

Fabio scrutinised Lucy's face while feeling her pulse. He straightened and smiled at Katie. 'She's okay. Rest is good. I'll let Amelia know where she is.'

'I'll stay with her until she wakes up,' Katie said. 'Tell Amelia not to worry.'

Fabio nodded his head in the direction of the balcony and Katie followed him outside. He closed the door behind them.

'It's important we let Lucy do whatever she

feels able to,' he said. 'It's what she wants. Understandably her parents would prefer to wrap her in cotton wool, but Lucy has let me know in no uncertain terms that she wants to be treated as if she were any child.

'She doesn't want us to treat her as if she's a patient,' he continued. 'She prefers to think of us as being friends of her parents, people who are here because they want to be, rather than because she's ill. I like to think of all my patients in terms of the family and not in isolation.'

That explained Fabio's informal and apparently casual attitude. Katie found herself revising her opinion of him once again.

'She's a brave girl,' Katie said. She looked around the marina, taking in the wealth all around. 'My guess is that her parents would give every penny they have to have her well.'

'And you'd be right. But they can't.' His expression relaxed. 'They're really glad to have you here, you know. They wouldn't have risked bringing Lucy out here unless they knew she could have professional physio on hand whenever she needs it. A lot of parents do the therapy themselves, but Amelia hates doing it. She's scared she hurts Lucy.'

'I can appreciate that, but I think we should encourage her to give it a go. I won't always be around to do Lucy's physio—at least, not as often as she needs it. Besides, once they learn how to do it and get confident, many parents become really good at it.'

He studied her as if he were truly seeing her for the first time and she shifted uncomfortably under the intensity of his gaze. 'You're a surprise, Katie Simpson, do you know that? I get the feeling that if anyone can persuade Amelia, it'll be you.' He looked as if he was about to add something but then he turned to leave. 'We'll be up on deck if you're looking for us,' he said.

By the time Katie had finished unpacking her few belongings and taken a shower, Lucy was awake again. Realising that her suit was totally inappropriate, Katie changed into a skirt and cotton blouse. They went back on deck to find Mark had returned and Fabio was chatting to both him and Amelia.

As soon as Amelia saw them, she rushed over to her daughter and hugged her tightly.

'Did you have a good sleep, sweetie?'

Lucy nodded. 'Katie let me use her bed.'

'Daddy is going back to the track to practise. Do you want to come and watch? Or would you rather stay here and wait to see him in the race?'

'Mummy, I said before, I'm coming and you're not to fuss,' Lucy said. 'I'm okay.' She softened her tone and smiled at her father. 'I can't wait to see Daddy practise.'

Mark scooped his daughter into his arms. 'And so you will. C'mon, then. Let's get going.'

The race track was only a short drive from the yacht, so close they could have walked, although it didn't seem to occur to anyone to do so. No doubt they were scared of tiring their daughter unnecessarily. As soon as Katie was out of the air-conditioned car, she smelled oil and rubber.

'Hey, Fabio. If you fancy a spin around the track, I'm sure I could arrange it.' Mark said.

Mark had to be kidding.

But Fabio didn't seem think so. A broad smile spread across his face. 'Fancy it? That's putting it mildly. I'd give my right arm for a go in one of those monsters you race.'

Mark laughed. 'I knew you'd be up for it. Okay, then, let's go and get you suited up.'

The two men left them to go and change.

'Can Mark do that?' Katie asked. 'I mean, let Fabio have a shot at driving the car? Surely there are rules?'

Amelia smiled. 'You'll soon learn that one thing neither Fabio nor my husband care about are rules. They're both adrenaline junkies.'

'So I heard on the plane,' Katie said. 'Lucy said that they met BASE jumping?'

'God, yes. I made Mark give it up as soon as I watched a video of him and Fabio doing it. It's a crazy sport. They throw themselves off these huge cliffs and wait until they're almost half-way down before they open their parachutes. So many people die, it's practically outlawed in some places.'

God, it sounded even more dangerous than Fabio had made out.

Lucy was skipping ahead of them, but to be on the safe side Katie lowered her voice.

'Aren't you scared something will happen to Mark when he's racing?'

Amelia's expression darkened. 'I'm terrified

every time he goes out on that track, believe me, but he wouldn't be the man I love if he didn't do what he does. I couldn't stop him anyway. All I can do is pray that he'll stay safe.' She smiled briefly. 'But it's not as dangerous as people think. At least all the cars are going in the same direction and there are ambulances and people with fire extinguishers on standby the whole time. On the whole, I'm happier with Mark racing than BASE jumping.' She shuddered. 'Now, *that* terrified me.'

It wasn't exactly reassuring. Having a husband who was a racing driver must be close to having a brother in the army in Afghanistan. Why was it that some men needed to face danger to feel alive? Didn't they realise the agony they put their loved ones through? But people didn't choose who they fell in love with. Amelia had still fallen for Mark despite his chosen career, and Suzy had never tried to stop Richard from doing the job he loved either.

Katie vowed that when she fell in love it would be with someone she knew she had a good chance of growing old with.

* * *

At the race track, they were made welcome. They were offered a seat in the viewing area and a cool drink, but Lucy was keen to visit the pits, so that was where they headed.

The area was crowded with mechanics fiddling with engines and chatting. Fabio and Mark were already there, suited up in similar overalls. Fabio looked in his element.

'I'd rather race,' he was saying to Mark. 'I know you'll beat me hands down but, hey, I'll never get another chance to race you again.'

'You wouldn't see me for dust, mate.' Mark's expression turned serious. 'These babies are worth a small fortune, Fabio, and with your track record you have to promise me you'll stay under a hundred and twenty. Keep behind me, but not too close. I don't want you taking me out by accident. And we're only doing two laps. Okay? Use the first to get used to how the car handles.'

A hundred and twenty! Were the pair of them out of their minds?

Fabio's eyes glittered. 'I'm not crazy, you know. I'll take it easy, I swear.'

The men were helped into the narrow cockpits of their separate cars. With his helmet on, only Fabio's eyes were visible. There was no mistaking the excitement in them. Katie seriously doubted he'd be able to keep himself or his car under control.

She was almost tempted to excuse herself—she really had no interest in watching her colleague fulfil a boyhood fantasy but for some reason she couldn't bring herself to leave.

The noise of the cars revving up would have been deafening had the staff not handed out ear defenders to everyone. With one final roar of the engines and the screech of burning rubber, the two men were off and within seconds had disappeared from view, already travelling at speed.

Less than two minutes later the cars came back into view, hurtling down the track towards them. Even with the sound muffled, Katie could still hear the tremendous whine of the engines, and she could feel the ground vibrating beneath her feet. The smell of burning fuel filled the air, adding to the sense of drama and excitement. Despite herself, Katie leant forward, hands clutched with tension as she tried to make out who was in front. As they roared past, Lucy was jumping up and down with excitement.

'Go, Daddy, go!'

Before Katie knew it, they were back and Fabio was climbing out of his car.

'Thanks, mate,' he said to Mark. ''That was some adrenaline rush. I wish I'd tried it sooner. Maybe I should take up rally driving instead.'

Fabio obviously had nerves of steel. He looked as unruffled as if he'd just been for a Sunday drive. Totally at ease in his black and red jump-suit, the helmet casually tucked under an arm, he oozed sex appeal. He caught her looking at him and dropped his lid in a wink. Her heart gave another awkward thump and she looked away quickly.

At least she had a colleague for a little while longer. But what was he thinking? They were here to work, not have fun.

Another roar of an engine and Mark was off again. Fabio turned to Amelia, Lucy and Katie.

'Your dad is some driver, isn't he, Luce?'

'He's the best,' Lucy agreed. 'I just know he's going to win the race.'

'Of course he will,' Fabio said. 'If you'll all excuse me, I'll go and get changed.'

'Why don't we get some lunch upstairs, Lucy?'

Amelia suggested. 'We'll be able to see Dad better from up there.' She turned to Katie. 'You'll join us? Mark'll be at least another couple of hours out on the track. They have to be sure the car is handling just right before the race.'

'When is it?' Katie asked.

'Tomorrow. Then he's off to Istanbul for the next one in a couple of weeks. Depending on how Lucy is, we might go to that one too. If you and Fabio are free to come too, that is?' Amelia watched her daughter who had skipped on ahead. 'You don't know how good it feels for us to be able to spend time as a family.' She paused and bit her lip. 'We don't know for sure how long Lucy might be with us, so we want to spend as much time together as possible.'

Katie touched her on the shoulder. 'Hopefully she'll be with you long enough to give you grey hairs. Children with CF are doing so much better now.' And she was being truthful. These days, around half of children with CF could expect to live to their late thirties and improvements in treatment meant that babies born today with the condition could expect to live much longer. In the 1960s a child was lucky to survive much beyond his or her fifth birthday. Of course, Amelia would know all that. Not that it was likely to be of much comfort. No parent would want to dwell on the fact that it was possible they would outlive their child.

After lunch, they all returned to the yacht. Lucy was due another round of physio.

Before Katie started, Fabio checked his small patient over.

'Chest sounds good, Luce,' he said, returning his stethoscope to his leather medical bag.

'Does that mean I can skip my physio?' Lucy asked hopefully.

'Nice try, kiddo. But you know it doesn't.'

'S'pose so. I need to use the bathroom first.'

While they waited for Lucy, Fabio turned to Katie. 'There's a drinks party this evening. I don't know if Amelia remembered to tell you.'

The thought of spending an evening with strangers panicked Katie. Especially as it would no doubt be crowded with the outrageously rich and famous glitterati of Monaco.

'I won't be expected to go, surely? If you don't mind, I'd much rather have something to eat in my room and an early night.' It wasn't just the thought of spending an evening with stars—she just didn't feel up to a party. Not that she wanted to share the real reason for her reluctance with Fabio.

'You don't have to stay long.' Fabio replied, leaning against her dressing table. 'You never know, you might even enjoy yourself.'

'I doubt it. It's just not my...scene.' Damn! That made her sound even more gauche and unsophisticated than she already felt.

'If you're worried about meeting some of the guests, believe me, they're all just ordinary people under their confident facades.'

'It's easy for you to say. You're used to this world. I'm not.' Oh, God, was he never going to give up? 'Anyway I didn't think to bring anything appropriate to wear.'

His look was appreciative. 'I think you could wear anything and still look good.'

Katie flushed. As soon as she found herself warming to him, he resorted to the playboy charm. It must come as natural to him as breathing.

'I'm sure Amelia will lend you a dress if need

be.' He looked at his watch and turned to go. 'I'll let Amelia and Mark know that Lucy will be along after she's rested.' Then, whistling, he left Katie standing in her room, unable to think of anything to say.

CHAPTER THREE

FABIO stood on the deck with a glass of freshly squeezed orange juice in his hand and looked around the crowd of partygoers. There was the usual mix of sports stars, singers and actors. He knew a lot of them from other occasions. Although he'd told Katie she would find the other guests interesting, in many ways he found it boring. It was the same old crowd, the same old parties, the same chat about who was dating who, who had clinched the bigger deal, whose career was on the up, and more salaciously whose was heading down.

He had thought about phoning the co-pilot and inviting her, but had decided against it. He was at work and didn't like to mix business with pleasure. He'd wait until he got back to the UK before he called her.

Then he saw Katie step onto the deck. Her blonde hair, unleashed from the plait, was gleaming gold in the moonlight. Her eyes were wide with excitement, or anxiety—he couldn't tell which, although he suspected the latter. As she stood on her own, separate from the crowd, twisting a lock of hair between her fingers, Fabio felt an unexpected rush of protectiveness.

A simple sundress exposed her delicate collarbones and revealed shapely, lightly tanned legs. Although she wore none of the ostentatiously expensive diamond jewellery the other women did and he knew enough about women's clothes to know that her dress was no designer one-off, she outshone every other female on the yacht. Next to her the others looked overdressed and unnatural. He was stunned. Was this the same woman he had travelled with? As if sensing his eyes on her, she found his gaze and in that split second it was as if everyone else disappeared.

He pushed his way through the crowd until he was by her side.

'So you decided to make an appearance after all?' he asked.

She smiled up at him, relief at having a familiar face to talk to evident in her grey eyes.

'Lucy made me. She said if I stayed in my room

she wouldn't come to the party either, so I promised I would come for a short while.'

Grabbing a glass of champagne from a passing waiter, Fabio passed it to Katie. She took it with a grateful smile. 'I still feel as if I don't belong.'

'Trust me, you're already attracting attention. From the women as much as the men. They're all wondering who you are. The men because they're planning how to move in on you and the women because they want to know who the competition is.'

'Don't be ridiculous.' She smiled at him and he felt the strangest feeling—one he didn't recognise—in the pit of his stomach.

'But I don't care if I do look like Cinderella. I'm here to do a job and if I have to join in, that's what I'll do.' Her smile grew wider and her eyes sparkled mischievously. 'I doubt I'll ever be as close to the rich and famous again, so I'm going to enjoy it. Now, won't you tell me who is who? I don't want to embarrass myself or offend anyone by not recognising people I perhaps should. Later, I'm going to write it all down in my diary so I can tell my grandchildren about it.'

Fabio's pulse was still behaving oddly. All of a

sudden he wanted nothing better than to be alone with Katie and find a corner where he could keep bringing that mischievous glint to her eyes. But he couldn't. They were both on duty. And…he groaned inwardly…she was a colleague. Hadn't he told himself earlier that an affair was out of the question? That it would only lead to trouble sooner or later? But that had been before, when he'd been sure she wasn't his type. Seeing her now was like a punch to his solar plexus.

He had to ignore the feeling in his gut, or at least he *should* ignore the feeling his gut. He wasn't at all sure he was going to be able to do so.

'Okay. See that couple over there?' He indicated a man and a woman who were surrounded by fawning admirers. 'You must recognise them. Every one in the world knows who they are.'

'Oh, my God, yes! They're on the front page of most newspapers. The golden husband and wife of the film world.' Katie replied. 'I just find it hard to believe that it's truly them and not a couple of look-alikes.'

'Come on, then, I'll introduce you.' He liked the way she wasn't scared to show her wonder.

Panic flared in her eyes and she shook her head. 'I'd rather not,' she protested. 'What on earth will I say to them?'

'I think you'll find that they are more than happy to have an audience,' Fabio said dryly, and taking her by the elbow guided her across to the couple.

As it turned out, Fabio was right. The couple were charming and did most of the talking. All Katie had to do was nod and smile in the right places. She'd been terrified when she'd first come up on deck. The yacht was packed with glamorous men and women: the women in designer gowns that shimmered as they moved, diamonds sparkling at throats and hands, or in shorter, figure-hugging dresses, exposing long golden limbs; the men in tuxedos, with crisp white shirts and bow-ties. Everywhere Katie looked she thought she recognised someone from the movies or television or the modelling world. Next to the expertly made-up women in their impossibly high designer heels, Katie felt completely underdressed in her last season's sundress, her face made up with only the merest slick of lipstick and mascara.

When she'd arrived, she had spotted Fabio immediately. Even next to the recognisable faces of well-known heartthrobs from the sporting and film world he'd stood out. Looking relaxed and assured in his dinner suit, his dark head bent to listen to something a flame-haired woman was whispering in his ear, he was the best-looking man on board. He must have felt her eyes on him because he looked up. Their eyes locked and her heart crashed against her ribs. Despite what she'd promised Lucy, she had been on the verge of hot footing it back to her cabin.

But before she could retreat, Fabio made a beeline towards her. Fleeing then would have made her look even more gauche than she already felt, and she was damned if she was going to let him see how unnerved she was, not only by the overwhelming number of beautiful people but the way the sight of him had stopped her breath. It had taken every ounce of her resolve to summon the smile she gave him.

Her heart was still pounding with excitement as the stars talked about their latest movies. If it hadn't been for the music coming from a string quartet, she was sure everyone would have heard it beating.

'Your cousin Kendrick was the stunt co-ordinator on set, you know,' Oliver Douglas, one half of the fabulous couple, was saying.

'And how is Kendrick?' Fabio asked.

'Crazy as ever. He keeps pushing the boundaries as far as stunts are concerned, and the directors love him for it. So do we, don't we, darling? It makes us, or at least me, look better.' Oliver smiled at his wife with a self-deprecating grin. 'We're just surprised he doesn't get hurt more often.'

'I guess as he didn't manage to get himself killed when he was in the army, he'll probably manage to keep himself in one piece on the set,' Fabio said dryly.

Oliver frowned. 'Didn't he fly helicopters in Iraq or Afghanistan? Is it true he almost got killed rescuing some men who were pinned down by enemy fire? I heard something went wrong. That he went against orders and his commanding officers weren't too pleased.'

'My cousin has never been one to let orders get in the way of doing what he feels is right,' Fabio said. Although his voice was quiet, almost gentle, there was a steely expression in his eyes.

Katie's blood ran cold. She didn't want to hear about the army. She didn't want to hear about war. She certainly didn't want to hear about rescue operations that went wrong. Couldn't they find something more pleasant to talk about? Their movies, for example. Their houses in exotic places. Anything except war. Images of her brother flooded her head. The two of them laughing at an old movie. He cajoling her to join him on a huge roller-coaster at a theme park, and laughing till he cried at how she'd screamed. Unlike her, he hadn't been frightened of anything.

Now he was dead. He hadn't been playing a part in a movie. He was gone and he was never coming back. As tears burned behind her lids, she clenched her teeth so hard it made her jaw ache. She needed to get away. There was no way she could contribute to this conversation. Her head was spinning, making her feel dizzy, and she swayed slightly. Would her feet even obey her commands?

Fabio was looking at her through narrowed

eyes. He took her by the elbow and steadied her. 'Would you excuse us? There's someone I have to introduce Katie to.'

Without giving the couple a chance to respond, Fabio steered Katie away towards a quiet area of the yacht. She gripped the rail tightly, trying to stop her hands trembling, taking deep breaths as she waited for the dizziness to pass.

'What is it, Katie?' Fabio asked. 'You look as if you've seen a ghost.'

Katie couldn't speak through her numb lips. She clenched her jaw, praying that tears wouldn't come. Not here, not in front of all these people, not in front of this man.

'You're shivering. Here.' Fabio took off his jacket and draped it around her shoulders. It smelled of him. Lemon and spice.

'Thanks,' she mumbled. She wished he would go away. Then she could slink back to her cabin and give in to the tears.

'Do you want to talk about it?' His voice was gentle.

Please, she thought, don't be nice to me. Anything else—flirt, whatever—just don't be kind. If he was kind, it would undo her.

She gave a vigorous shake of her head.

'Okay, then, I'll do the talking for a while.' He indicated a man well over six feet five with silver hair, who was leaning nonchalantly against a polished railing. 'See him? Do you know he used to be a baseball star before going into the movies?'

Fabio stood next to her, not quite touching, but almost. He carried on, his voice calm and soothing, until eventually she felt some of the tension leave her body.

'And the red-haired woman in the black dress?' He tipped his head in the direction of a film star who had been nominated for several awards. 'I heard tonight that's she's planning to divorce husband number five. I can't imagine marrying once, let alone five times!' He kept pointing people out, dropping in little bits of gossip and wry remarks until Katie had to smile.

'That's better,' he said, noticing.

'Thanks for staying with me.' She cleared her throat. 'And thanks for not asking me any questions. I'm going to go back downstairs and check on Lucy.' She shrugged out of his jacket and held it out to him. 'Please, go back to the party. I've monopolised you enough.'

He tipped her chin and looked into her eyes. 'I'd rather stay with you. I can party anytime.'

The touch of his fingertip on her skin sent a spark down her spine. How could she go from thinking her heart was breaking to feeling like this all in a matter of a few minutes? How could this man have such an effect on her?

'No, please. I'm really tired, Fabio, but thanks.'

His eyes glinted in the moonlight. He leaned towards her and for one heart-stopping moment Katie thought he was going to kiss her. Instead, he brushed his lips against her forehead. It was just the lightest of pressure but enough to send a flash of heat through her.

'Sleep tight. I'll see you in the morning,' he said lightly, before walking away.

Katie was rooted to the spot as she watched him disappear into the crowd. Although she barely knew him, he was making her feel as if he was pulling her into his orbit, from where there would be no escape.

CHAPTER FOUR

THE next day everyone was up early and Katie found them all gathered for breakfast on deck.

A white-uniformed crew member pulled out her chair for her and asked her what she would like to eat. Katie looked at the side table, which was groaning with platters of fruit, pastries and cheese and cold meats.

'Coffee and a couple of those delicious-looking pastries, please,' she said.

Fabio was reading the paper, clearly having long since finished his breakfast, and looked up in surprise.

'I know I shouldn't,' she said defensively. 'But they just look so good.'

'Hey, I like a woman who enjoys eating. Most of the women I know, with the exception of you, Amelia, barely consume enough calories to keep themselves alive.'

The grin he gave her made her heart thump.

She had been feeling anxious about seeing him after almost making a fool of herself the evening before, but he was clearly happy to pretend nothing out of the ordinary had happened and she was grateful to him.

Last night had been the first time she had slept without waking with tears on her pillow. Instead she had slept soundly, dreaming of dark green eyes and a full mouth. God, she realised, feeling a warmth rush through her body, she had been dreaming of being held in his arms, of him kissing her with a ferocity that made her heart sing. She looked away, terrified he could read her mind.

Even though she had clearly lost it. The dream had been so erotic—and so real—it made her blush to remember it. Perhaps it was transference or whatever it was called. Fabio had been so kind, staying with her until she'd got herself together—never mind what he must have thought of her odd behaviour the evening before. She cringed inwardly. So much for presenting a professional front at all times. The last thing she wanted was for him to think that she wasn't up to the job.

Avoiding his eyes, she looked out to sea. The

sun bounced off the water, making it sparkle. To her surprise the yacht was no longer moored. Some time through the night it had moved from the marina out into the bay.

'Daddy races today, but not until this afternoon,' Lucy said. 'Mummy and I are going to stay on board this morning.' Lucy looked contented with her world.

'We thought Fabio could show you around the town. Would you like that?' Amelia suggested, smiling at her daughter.

Katie glanced at Fabio, uncertain. After last night and her dream, she felt shy and awkward in his presence.

'Shouldn't we stay here?' she asked.

'I'm sure Amelia and Lucy would be glad of some time together,' Fabio said. 'But I'm sure they won't mind if you want to stay and sunbathe. You can swim from the side of the yacht if you like.'

'Or you can do both,' Amelia said. 'Have a dip, then go and see a bit of Monaco before the race. It's entirely up to you.'

Katie stared across at the clear blue water. The

thought of cooling off was extremely appealing. There was only one problem.

'I didn't think to bring my bikini,' she said. 'It didn't occur to me.'

Amelia smiled. 'Luckily I have a drawer full.' She eyed Katie. 'You and I are about the same size. You're a bit shorter and smaller, but I don't think there's much in it.'

Fabio was studying Katie speculatively. 'Didn't you tell me you swim every day? I wouldn't mind a swim myself and I'm sure Lucy will join us.'

'C'mon, Katie.' Lucy added her entreaties. 'Mummy doesn't like to swim and it'll be more fun if you and Fabio come in too.'

'Okay, then.' Katie gave in. Exercise was good for Lucy.

After breakfast, Amelia helped Katie select a bikini. Although they were all more beautiful than anything Katie had ever worn, they all seemed slightly on the skimpy side, but seeing that she had no real choice she chose one that appeared to offer the most coverage.

By the time she'd changed and come back on deck, Lucy and Fabio were already in the water.

'C'mon, Katie,' Lucy implored. 'We're waiting for you.'

Fabio was treading water. With his dark hair slicked down with the water, he looked different—more vulnerable, more human. And, if it were possible, even more sexy.

'Yes, *vamos*. Or do I have to come up there and get you?' he threatened with a glint in his eye.

Katie had no doubt he would do as he said. She balanced on the edge of the yacht and taking a deep breath dived straight in. She gasped as she hit the cool water, but moments later it felt deliciously cool and refreshing.

She bobbed up within inches of Fabio. He was still looking at her with a gleam in his eyes. 'That was some dive,' he said appreciatively. His expression grew serious. 'Are you okay?' he said. His genuine look of concern rattled her. She didn't want him to think she needed looking after. Last night had been a glitch. In future she'd be more careful to keep her feelings under control.

'I'm fine. I was tired, that's all. It was a long day,' she replied, keeping her voice matter-of-fact.

He looked at her searchingly for a moment. She was sure he didn't believe her. Then, as if he knew he wouldn't get more from her, the teasing look was back in his eyes.

'Want to race?' he said.

Lucy had eased herself onto an airbed and was paddling towards them.

'If you race, I'll be the judge,' she offered.

Katie was about to refuse when she read the challenge in Fabio's eyes. Her heart started pounding.

'Okay.' She pointed to a buoy in the distance. 'What about to that marker and back?'

'Done. I'll give you a head start if you like,' Fabio said with a smile.

'Not needed.' Katie retorted.

'Okay, ready, steady, go!' Lucy shouted, cupping her hands around her mouth.

Without waiting to see what Fabio was up to, Katie set off at a fast crawl. Each time she lifted her face to the side to suck in some air, she looked for him, but he was nowhere in sight. Good. She must be in front. But when she touched the buoy, she saw that he had been ahead of her and was turning back already. Damn. She increased her speed, putting every ounce of energy into making her legs and arms move faster. Soon she was alongside him, and then with a last effort past him. That would show him.

But just as Lucy, and the finishing line, was within easy reach, a hand grabbed her foot and she was tugged under.

Twisting out of his grip, Katie bobbed to the surface. Fabio had started swimming away from her and would easily cross the finishing line before her. The cheat! Well, two could play at that game and perhaps it would convince him that her emotional wobble the evening before was well and truly in the past. With a wink at Lucy, she let out a loud yelp and pretended to grab at her calf.

Fabio stopped swimming and turned towards her. He frowned when he saw the fake agony on her face. 'Katie! What's wrong?'

'Cramp,' Katie groaned, sliding a look at Lucy, who hid her giggles behind her hand.

Fabio swam back towards her and his arm snaked around her waist. 'Hold onto me,' he said. The heat of his bare skin against hers was send-ing little bolts of electricity shooting through her, almost making her forget about the race. For a moment the world stood still as she looked into his heavily lashed eyes. Confused by the sensations running through her, Katie pulled away. 'Got you!' she yelled triumphantly. Kicking her legs as fast as she could, she swam towards Lucy. She ignored Fabio's shout behind her, aware that if she stopped even for a second he would catch up.

'I win!' Her ruse had worked. She grinned as Lucy high-fived her.

When Fabio arrived seconds behind her his expression was dark and dangerous. Katie's pulse beat even faster.

Lucy slipped back in the water and swam away.

'You cheated,' he said.

'You cheated first!'

'Ah, but winning is all that matters,' he drawled. 'At least as far as I'm concerned. I should warn you, I don't believe in rules.'

He was still looking at her as if he was contemplating what to do to her. Her heart was behaving as if someone was drumming out a rock song on it.

'Maybe you don't know me as well as you think,' she said. Now she was flirting back.

Once more Katie was acutely conscious of Fabio's nearly naked body only inches from hers, and to her dismay, something that felt very close to lust curled in her pelvis.

'I...I should go after Lucy,' she managed, mortifyingly aware that her voice was husky.

The way Fabio was looking at her suggested he knew exactly what effect he was having on her. Damn the man and his gorgeousness.

'She's fine, Katie,' he murmured, holding her gaze, his eyes sparking with mischief. 'Payback time.'

His arms shot out and holding her tightly against him he sank with her beneath the surface of the water. She fought to wriggle free, every thrust of her body bringing her closer against him and adding to the clamour of sensations sweeping through her. When they bobbed back to the surface, something shifted in Fabio's eyes and his grin faded. Knowing she had to get away from him, Katie pushed him away and swam towards the yacht as if the hounds from hell were snapping at her heels. By the time she arrived next to

Lucy she was breathless and she knew it wasn't from swimming.

While she and Lucy splashed in the water, Katie watched her patient carefully for any signs of breathing difficulty. There were none.

Having taken possession of the airbed, Fabio lay on his stomach, using his hands to propel his way towards them.

When he reached them, he turned over and lay on his back, shielding his eyes from the sun with his hand.

Katie and Lucy looked at each other and with one accord they ducked under the water and came up next to him, pushing over his makeshift sunbed and tipping him into the water.

Fabio came up gasping and shaking the water from his eyes. He gave Katie and Lucy a wicked grin, before grabbing the child and tossing her into the air.

Then his hands spanned Katie's waist.

His touch sent her already thumping heart rate into overdrive and she found herself looking into his eyes, almost unable to breathe again. His mouth was inches away from hers. Was he going to kiss her this time? She couldn't move, couldn't breathe. But then with a look of what she could have sworn was regret he dropped his hands.

'We'd better get back to the yacht.'

Dismayed at the thud of disappointment she felt, Katie could only nod.

Back on board, Lucy went to have a rest while Katie changed into denim shorts and a white cotton shirt. For the first time in as long as she could remember, she felt almost light-hearted. The morning had been fun—if unsettling. Back there, in the water, when Fabio had held her, she'd had the strangest sensation of coming home, which was crazy. Men like Fabio were heart-breakers and she needed to remember that. Her heart was in bad enough condition as it was—the last thing she needed was more pain.

Back on deck, Fabio had also changed, his short-sleeved white shirt emphasising his bronzed chest.

'Are you ready for lunch ashore?' he asked. Katie was perplexed. The yacht was still out in the bay and she wondered how they were supposed to get there. Surely Fabio didn't expect them to swim?

'There's a little boat we can use,' Fabio said, as if reading her mind. 'The crew are happy for me to take us, if you trust me, that is?'

No, she didn't. Not after that morning. But even Fabio couldn't get up to any mischief in the short distance to shore. Or so she thought.

The small boat wasn't small at all. It was a rubber dinghy but one with a powerful outboard motor. Fabio suggested she sit behind him at the wheel and she did so, trying to keep as much distance between her body and his as was possible on the narrow seat, but when he revved up the engine so hard it almost reared in the air Katie squealed and wrapped her arms around his waist, acutely conscious of the hard muscles of his abdomen under her fingertips.

Instead of turning towards the shore, Fabio headed further out to sea and opened the throttle. Soon they were bouncing along like a bucking bronco on the waves.

Resigned, Katie gave herself up to the sensation of speed and the wind in her hair. As they scooted over the waves, she let herself enjoy feeling free and happy. It had been so long since she'd felt that way.

Eventually Fabio turned the boat round and headed towards land.

He turned to grin at her. 'Sorry. Just couldn't resist giving her a little run. You didn't get wet, did you?'

Katie's legs were like jelly as she stepped ashore, but whether it was because of the adrenaline rushing through her body or because of the memory of Fabio's body against hers, she didn't want to think about. Did this man have to live every minute in the fast lane? Was he ever happy to be at peace?

At least there was little he could do to agitate her as they walked in companionable silence around Monaco. The shops were amazing. Filled with clothes and jewellery that didn't deign to have price tags, Katie guessed that if anyone needed to ask the price they couldn't afford it.

'It's all kind of make-believe,' she said finally. 'Almost like a film set. Everything about this trip feels unreal.'

Fabio studied her through half-closed eyes, a small smile playing on his lips. 'Don't you like it?' he asked.

Katie thought for a moment. 'It is beautiful but,

no. I don't think I'd feel comfortable living here. I think being surrounded by so much wealth all the time feels a little obscene when there's so much poverty in the world. What about you?'

Fabio looked thoughtful. 'I always thought I liked it, but I understand what you mean about not wanting to live here. As for the wealth and it being obscene, I feel like that sometimes about Brazil. People there are either enormously rich or pretty impoverished. Not easy to live with.' His words surprised her. He seemed so comfortable with the rich and glamorous lifestyle.

Fabio stopped next to some tables and chairs of an outside café and raised an eyebrow. 'Ready to eat?'

'I'm okay. But something cool to drink would be good.'

Unsurprisingly, there were no prices on the menu. After they had ordered their drinks, Katie leaned back in her seat and turned her face to the sun.

'Tell me more about Brazil,' she said. 'Is there really such a divide?'

Fabio nodded. 'I wasn't aware of it until I qualified as a doctor. I spent a year working in the inner city and it opened my eyes. Maybe one day, I'll go back and work there again.'

Katie regarded him through half-closed eyes. 'What? And leave all this?' She indicted the square with its magnificent fountain and the immaculate buildings with a wave of her hand. 'All this luxury?' Could he be pretending to be something he wasn't in order to impress her? If that was the case, she didn't know whether to be flattered or annoyed. She was in a state of constant confusion around him. One minute his natural mode of operating seemed to be to flirt with every woman he met—she had no illusions she was special in any way—although when she was with him he made her feel as if she was the only woman on the planet. On the other hand, he seemed to genuinely care about Lucy and her family. She sighed inwardly. Men like him were beyond her scope of understanding.

The sun was warm on her face but a gentle breeze coming off the sea kept it from being too hot. She closed her eyes again, breathing in the scent from the baskets of flowers and taking in the sounds, content to feel at peace, even if only for a little while.

* * *

Fabio sipped his coffee and studied the woman opposite him. When he'd seen her poised at the side of the boat in her borrowed bikini, the sight of her had blown him away. Her petite figure was just as curvaceous as her sundress the night before had suggested. She had tied back her blonde hair in a ponytail, exaggerating her high cheekbones, and when she had dived into the sea, he had caught a glimpse of her sexily rounded bottom emphasised by the high cut of the bikini.

It wasn't just that she was sexy and cute in way that made him want to kiss her senseless. He loved watching her in her unguarded moments when her eyes would light up with wonder at everything she saw, although he believed her when she said it wasn't for her. Every moment he spent with her, she intrigued him more and more. Most of the women he dated were only too happy to talk about themselves, but not Katie. What caused that sad look in her eyes when she thought she wasn't being watched? The one that made him want to make her laugh instead? And why had she become so upset last night? What secrets did she have? He wanted to know.

He gave himself a slight shake. He had to remember that she was out of bounds. He was pretty certain women like Katie weren't into casual relationships. When they fell in love it was for ever, and one thing he could never promise was a happy ever after.

Later that day, after they'd watched Mark's race, which to everyone's delight he had won, and they were back on the yacht, Fabio checked Lucy over. Announcing himself satisfied, he left Katie to give Lucy her physio. Katie organised some pillows on the deck to do postural drainage.

'Isn't it great that Dad came first?' Lucy said. 'I wish I could have gone to the party with them.'

They'd all been invited, but Katie had opted to stay behind with Lucy. Fabio reappeared, wearing a dinner suit and bow-tie, just in time to catch Lucy's words.

'I think you've had enough excitement for the day. We all have,' Katie told Lucy.

'I'm too excited to go to bed. Can't I stay up? We could all play a board game. You, me and Fabio.'

'I think Fabio is going to the party, Luce.' Katie glanced at Fabio, suppressing a smile as she saw the fleeting look of horror on his face. No doubt staying in and playing a board game was as far away from a night out as was possible for him.

But to her surprise, Fabio loosened his bow-tie and shrugged out of his jacket.

'Sounds cool. I'm sure your folks won't mind me not going, Lucy. I'll let them know and I'll meet you ladies in the lounge.'

Realising her jaw had dropped, Katie quickly recovered. This was more like the behaviour she expected from Lucy's doctor, although, to be fair, participating in a board game went beyond the call of duty. She decided to ignore the little surge of pleasure she felt that he'd chosen to spend the evening with her and Lucy instead of at some glamorous event.

The three of them gathered round the coffee table, sitting on piles of cushions scattered over the thick pile rug. Soft lamps glowed in the corners and the lights of Monaco twinkled outside in the distance. For the first time in a long, long while, Katie felt almost happy.

'No cheating this time, Fabio.' Lucy giggled. 'Katie and I are on to you.'

Fabio mimed shocked horror. 'I'm a genius at Scrabble! I don't need to cheat.'

Lucy's first word scored eleven, Katie's nineteen and, much to their delight, Fabio's five. The next few rounds saw him lag even further behind, until he pulled a big word score out of nowhere.

'Hey! What does that word mean?' Lucy asked, suspicious.

'It's Portuguese,' Fabio replied, doing his best to look innocent. 'It's a term for a beautiful woman.'

Katie and Lucy nodded at each other. 'Get out the dictionary!' they shouted in unison. Lucy looked up 'quezob'. 'Nice try, Dr Fabio, but no such word exists.'

The rest of the game descended into a chaos of laughter as they all vied to win by cheating and using the most outrageous made-up words.

Finally, Fabio held up his hands in submission. 'I surrender—I can't compete with you two ganging up on me.'

'I think it's time for bed, Luce,' Katie said a short while later, noticing how tired the girl looked suddenly. A yawning Lucy allowed Katie to lead her away to bed, where Katie left her sleepily watching a movie.

When Katie returned to the lounge, she hesitated at the door. Fabio was sitting on the floor, leaning against one of the sofas with his arms behind his head. How could anyone seem so relaxed yet like a coiled spring at the same time? He was a mass of contradictions. Part of her wanted his company, but being alone with him suddenly seemed too intimate; too intense.

He jumped to his feet when he noticed her. For a moment they stood looking at each other and Katie's heart kicked against her ribs. He stepped towards her.

'I think I'll follow Lucy's example and have an early night,' she said, backing away quickly. His expression was unreadable.

'Did you have a good day?' His voice was low as if her answer really mattered to him.

'It's been wonderful.' She sounded breathless, even to her own ears. 'Goodnight, Fabio.'

But once in her bed, sleep evaded her. She was feeling very restless. Slipping on her dressing gown, she stepped outside her cabin and onto the balcony.

'Hello.' His voice came out of the darkness. 'Couldn't sleep?'

Fabio was sitting on his balcony, leaning back in his chair with his long legs propped up on the railings. Her heart started its annoying thumping all over again. If it wouldn't have looked crazy for her to head straight back inside, she would have.

She shook her head. 'No. I thought some air would help.'

'How is Lucy?'

'Fast asleep. Tired out from her day.'

'She's a good kid.' Fabio stood up and leaned his back against the railing so he was facing her.

'My heart goes out to her and her parents. I don't know how they manage to keep everything so normal. If this can be called normal.' Katie indicated the sweep of the marina with the thousand lights sparkling from the hundreds of yachts.

'It's normal for them. Don't let all of this fool you, Katie. Amelia and Mark love their daughter very much. They won't have any more children because they can't take the risk of having another child with CF. They both have to be carriers for Lucy to have inherited the illness in the first place and they have a one in four chance of having another child with CF. It's not a risk they're prepared to take I suspect they'd swap places with you in a heartbeat.'

She sucked in a breath. Would they? At least, for the time being, *their* family was safe and together.

'Maybe, maybe not,' she replied. As soon as the words were out she could have bitten her tongue. God, that sounded callous.

Fabio vaulted over the railing, joining her on her side of the balcony. He was so close she could smell his expensive aftershave, almost feel the heat of his body. Her heart went into overdrive. Why couldn't he have stayed where he was?

He tilted her chin gently so he could hold her gaze. 'Something is making you sad. Do you want to tell me what it is?'

Katie shook her head and stepped away. She wasn't ready to share what had happened to Richard with anyone, least of all him. Keeping everything locked up inside was the only way she knew how to cope with her grief. She was terrified that once the floodgates opened, she'd fall apart.

'I don't think it's something you'd want to hear about,' she said quietly.

'Don't judge me too quickly, Katie.' Although his tone was light, his expression was deadly serious.

He seemed so sincere, she found herself wanting to confide in him. But talking about it wouldn't change anything. It wouldn't bring Richard back. And Fabio was a colleague. One she barely knew. She'd already revealed more to him than she wanted to. 'Thanks, but I'm fine, Fabio.'

He took a step towards her and her heart almost stopped beating. For a moment it was as if she was being held in his arms and he wasn't even touching her. She needed to keep her distance from this man in more ways than one.

'I'll see you in the morning,' she said, and before he had a chance to respond, she was back inside her cabin.

Back on his side of the balcony, Fabio stared up at the sky. Katie wasn't the only one who was struggling to find sleep that night. Perhaps it was because he couldn't stop thinking about her. Which was ridiculous.

Wasn't it?

Why was he letting her get under his skin? Okay, so something was upsetting her, but that wasn't his problem. There was no reason on this earth that he should feel this sense of protectiveness. No reason at all that he should keep imagining the feel of her lips, the touch of her fingers, the sensation of her hair on his chest, the swell of her hips under his hand. No reason why he should be remembering her bare skin with little droplets of water rolling down between her breasts.

He had almost kissed her back there and if she hadn't turned away, he would have. Even if he knew he was playing with fire. *Deus!* There were plenty of women he could be dating. Women equally as beautiful and far less complicated. So why didn't any of them make his pulse beat the way Katie did?

Fabio stood up and with his hands thrust into his pockets paced the small balcony. He'd had a surprisingly good time earlier that evening. Who would ever have thought that Fabio Lineham would enjoy playing Scrabble with Katie and Lucy more than any other date he could remember in the last year? He chuckled as he remembered the heated look on Katie's face when she'd caught him cheating. The impish smile as she'd tried to get her own back by nudging his letters away from the triple-score square.

At one point, when Katie had been frowning over her letters, it had struck him that this what being part of a family must be like for most people, and for the first time in his adult life he'd experienced a stab of envy.

He had to stop thinking like that. He had to get Katie out of his head and there was only one sure-fire way left to cure himself of his desire for her. As the thought flashed through his head, he felt an unexpected prickle of shame but quickly dismissed it. She would have to take her chances.

CHAPTER FIVE

THE flight back home to London was uneventful, except that this time Amelia was with them. A car picked them up and, after dropping off Amelia and Lucy, along with Fabio who said he wanted to give Lucy a quick once-over at their mansion, carried on towards the part of London where Katie was staying with her sister-in-law.

Katie stood at the front door of the little maisonette in the gathering darkness and took a deep, steadying breath. Richard and Suzy had only moved in eighteen months ago and she still remembered how excited they'd both been with their first home. As soon as they'd decorated, they'd announced they were trying for a baby and they had both been so happy when Suzy's pregnancy had been confirmed. How could they have known that less than a year later it would all fall apart?

Swallowing the lump in her throat and plastering a smile on her face, Katie let herself in.

She wasn't surprised to find that her sister-in-law was still up, little Rick cradled in her arms.

'Oh, hi,' Suzy said lethargically. She was clutching a crumpled letter in her hand. 'How was your trip?'

Katie felt a rush of sympathy and immediately dismissed her own fatigue. 'I'll put this little one down, shall I, and make us a snack, then tell you all about it,' she said, holding out her arms for her nephew.

Gently, Katie removed the sleeping baby from Suzy's arms. She breathed in the particular baby smell and her heart contracted as two small eyes, exact replicas of his dead father's, opened and fixed on hers. Recognising his aunt, Ricky fell back to sleep.

She put him down in his cot and returned to the sitting room. Suzy was still sitting in the same position as when Katie had left her.

'His commanding officer wrote to me.' She waved the pages of the letter listlessly. 'He's going to recommend him for some medal. As if that would make things better.'

A crushing sense of guilt threatened to over-whelm Katie. If Richard hadn't needed the money to support her as well as himself, he would have never joined the army. But that wasn't all. When Richard had been offered the chance to serve abroad, before he'd fallen in love with Suzy, he'd come to Katie and asked her what he should do.

'I don't want to leave you on your own, kiddo,' he'd said. 'But this is something I need to do.'

'Hey, I'm all grown up now. I'll be fine,' she'd said, although she'd wanted to beg him not to go. He had looked after her practically all his adult life, supporting her, encouraging her to follow her dreams, and it had only been fair that she should let him follow his.

Crouching by her sister-in-law's side, Katie took the pages and read. As Suzy had said, Richard's commanding officer was recommending Richard for a medal. It was pretty much as they'd been told. Her brother had been stationed at a forward operating post when some of the soldiers under his care had come under fire. Without regard for his own safety, Richard had left the protection of the FOB and rushed out to pull one of the in-jured soldiers to safety. Then he had gone back for another. It had been at that point he had been shot and killed.

'I'm so angry with him,' Suzy said softly. 'I know it sounds crazy, but he was a doctor, not a soldier. He didn't have to do what he did.'

Katie rested her head against Suzy's shoulder.

'He had us to come home to,' Suzy continued. 'All he had to do was keep himself safe for another two weeks then he would have been back where he belonged. Here. With his family.'

'I know,' Katie said.

Suzy sighed deeply. 'But he wouldn't have been Richard, would he, if he hadn't done what he did? He wouldn't have been the man I loved. Whatever you think, Katie, Richard wouldn't have been happy doing anything else.'

Her words were an echo of Amelia's. A reminder that loving brought pain and that you couldn't help who you fell in love with. An image of Fabio floated into Katie's head. In many ways he reminded her of Richard. He had that same insatiable desire for excitement and danger as her brother had had. However much he made her nerve endings tingle, however much she was drawn to him, she had to remember he wasn't the man for her. For all sorts of reasons.

Tears were running down Suzy's cheeks and Katie knew that, despite her best efforts to be strong for her sister-in-law, her own cheeks were wet.

'Oh, Katie, how am I going to live without him?' Suzy wailed.

And then the two women were in each other's arms, seeking comfort that they knew they could never find.

When they had dried their tears and made some tea, they made themselves comfortable on the sofa.

'So tell me about your trip. Was it fun?' Suzy said.

Suzy was always trying to get Katie to get out and start enjoying life again, so Katie told Suzy about the yacht, Monaco and the people she had met. She tried to make her stories as amusing as possible and was rewarded when Suzy laughed.

'And this Dr Lineham—Fabio? Tell me more about him. I'm guessing he's gorgeous. Your eyes light up every time you mention him.'

Suzy had always been too perceptive for her own good. Katie felt her cheeks redden.

'He's good looking, but not my type.' She went on to tell Suzy about Fabio and the race with Mark. 'He also BASE jumps, which as far as I can gather is one of the most dangerous sports a person can do. So put any matchmaking thoughts out of your head. When I fall for someone, it's going to be a man whose idea of a crazy risk is doing the lottery once a week.'

Suzy laughed. 'I wonder.' Then her expression grew serious. 'You know Richard wrote to me not long before he died and said that if anything ever happened to him, I was to move on with my life, and that's what I'm trying to do. Oh, I'll never forget him and I doubt I'll ever love again, but I have Ricky to live for. But apart from Ricky and I, the person Richard cared about most, Katie, was you. He'd want to know you were happy. He'd want you to live your life to the full. Maybe this Fabio is a chance for you to move on with your life.'

Katie hugged her knees to her chest. 'He's a risk-taker, Suzy, and that's only one of many reasons there could never be anything between us. Even if he wanted there to be, which I very much doubt. He has that same reckless streak that Richard had.' Katie's breath caught. 'If only Richard hadn't joined the army because of me, he would still be alive.'

Suzy had never once blamed her for Richard being in the army. Never once given any indication that she held her responsible for Richard's death. Katie had tried to tell her how she felt, but Suzy had refused to listen.

'You have to stop blaming yourself, Katie,' Suzy said. 'Richard was born needing to challenge himself, and that's why I know the army was the right place for him. Even if it hadn't been a way to put himself through medical school while supporting you, I think Richard would have found a way to be in the army one way or another. He was an adrenaline junkie before he joined the forces. You have to stop tearing yourself into tiny pieces.'

Although Suzy meant what she said, and even if, deep down, Katie knew her guilt was illogical, she'd never stop feeling that some of the responsibility for Richard's death lay at her feet.

Katie reached for Suzy's hand. 'I couldn't put

myself through the endless worry all over again. I couldn't be you, or Amelia for that matter, never knowing whether today is the day you get the call you dread. I've lost three people I love much too soon and I'm not going to risk having my heart ripped out again.' She sighed. 'I don't know how you go on, left alone to bring up your baby.'

'I have Ricky and you and my parents, Katie. I have every reason to live. Loving Richard was the best thing that ever happened to me, even though losing him broke me into little pieces. Fabio may or may not be the right man for you, Katie, but at least promise me that you'll open your heart to the possibility of falling in love one day, whatever joy and sorrow that might bring.'

Katie managed a wobbly smile. 'I promise. Just as long as you know it won't be with Dr Fabio Lineham.'

Katie looked over her list of patients for the day. It was an easy schedule, a couple of footballers and an Olympic swimming hopeful who were coming to the practice for their physio. In the afternoon she had a home visit scheduled to an elderly patient who was recovering from a stroke and couldn't make it to the practice.

Even her experience of Monaco hadn't prepared her for the number of celebrities, sport stars and aristocracy that came through the doors.

When she'd come for her interview a couple of weeks earlier she'd known immediately that this was no ordinary practice. To begin with, instead of a formal interview with one or two of the most senior doctors sitting opposite her behind a desk, all of the staff had been there, seated comfortably in armchairs. Dr Cavendish, the senior partner, a suave, elegantly dressed man in his early thirties who looked happy with his lot in life; his wife Rose, who was currently heavily pregnant and who was one of the nurses as well as the practice manager; the receptionist, a lively-looking girl called Jenny in her late teens or early twenties with a startling haircut and a tattoo; and, finally, Vicki, the other nurse. The only one missing had been Fabio.

They had all gone out of their way to make her feel part of their small team and, Fabio notwithstanding, Katie was enjoying working there.

The footballers, whose names she didn't recognise but who caused a flutter with Jenny, arrived first. Katie ignored their teasing as she gave them their physio. It soon transpired that one was married and more than happy to exchange small talk about his wife and children as Katie worked on him. The other asked her to dinner, and seemed genuinely put out when Katie said no. No doubt he wasn't used to being refused. Tough. He was a patient and, besides, Katie instinctively knew that he was trouble. Nevertheless, she framed her refusal in a way that wouldn't cause offence. However, she had to admit it was good for her ego to be asked out.

Her next patient wasn't as straightforward as Katie had hoped. Gillian Blake had been pre-selected for the British Olympic swimming team and had a punishing schedule.

'I get up at five every day,' she told Katie, as Katie put her limbs through a series of passive movements, 'swim for six hours, come home, have something to eat, relax for an hour or two, then it's off to the gym for another couple of hours. It's great that you're here now. Before this, I had to go all the way across London for my physio. As you can imagine, that ate up a chunk of the day.'

'I like swimming too,' Katie told her, 'but my efforts amount to thirty laps at the most in the pool before or after work. It's the way I switch off from the world. I can't imagine doing it for hours and hours, every day of my life.'

'It's what I have to do if I want to stand a chance of getting a medal,' Gillian said. 'Thank goodness for the sports council grant. Now I can get some proper back-up to my training.'

Katie's hands paused at Gillian's knees. There was slight swelling and it felt hot to the touch.

'Gillian, have you injured your knee recently?' she asked.

The Olympic medal hopeful shook her head. 'No. At least, I didn't think I had. But it's been a bit sore over the last couple of months. It aches for a couple of days then the pain goes away. I wondered if there was something wrong with my technique. I asked my coach and he said no. It was him who suggested I come for a bit of physio and massage. It's probably overuse.'

'Mmm,' Katie said. 'Too much training could be the problem, but to be on the safe side I'd like one of the doctors to check you over. Would you be okay with that?'

Gillian frowned. 'I really don't think there's anything to worry about.' But Katie could see the doubt in her eyes.

'Let's just say I'd be happier if one of them had a look. You lie here and relax for a few minutes and I'll go and see who's free.'

Katie tapped on Fabio's door after checking with Jenny that he was alone. He had his feet up on the desk and was leaning back with his hands behind his head.

He leaped to his feet when she came in. What-ever else she thought about him, he had good manners, although she wished he wouldn't do that jumping-up thing every time she entered the room. It really was quite unnerving.

'Katie, what brings you into the lion's den?'

She wished he wouldn't take that flippant tone either. Since they'd returned from Monaco she had gone out of her way to avoid him, preferring to go to Jonathan Cavendish when she needed a medical opinion. She hoped that time would cure her of the peculiar way Fabio made her feel whenever he was around, particularly when they were alone. Unfortunately, today Jonathan had gone out to see a patient. Not that she could always avoid Fabio. She just had to keep their encounters on a professional footing.

'I'm with a patient at the moment. She's a swimmer who's hoping to win a medal in the games.'

His eyes had lost that sleepy look. He was immediately alert. When he wasn't assuming his cat-like repose position, he was like a curled up spring. Was there no happy medium with this man? 'Something's bothering you?'

'Yes. When I was doing her physio I noticed some swelling of her right knee. It's hot to the touch as well.'

'What are you thinking?'

'I'm thinking that there might be something going on with her. Like rheumatoid arthritis. I know it's a bit of a leap, but I wondered if you'd mind having a look. I don't want to take any chances.'

'Sure. No problem. My next patient isn't due for another ten minutes and she's always late anyway. C'mon—let's go and see your girl.'

She had to admire the way patients responded to Fabio. When he was with a patient he lost that teasing predator look and became the consummate professional. Not that he lost any of his charm—it was just that he was good at putting patients at ease.

When she noticed his eyes narrow almost imperceptibly as he examined Gillian's knee, after asking her searching questions about her general health, she knew she had been right to call him.

He hid his concern from his patient. 'I would like to take some blood for testing if that's okay, Gillian.'

Gillian sat up on the couch, looking alarmed. 'Why? What do you think is wrong? As I said to Katie, I'm sure it's no more than overuse. I'll cut back on practice a little and you'll see—the stiffness will go away.'

'You could well be right,' Fabio said evenly. 'But isn't it better to get these things checked out properly? Especially for athletes. Why don't I send some samples of blood to the lab and we can arrange for you to come back and see me in a day or two. That way we can all be reassured.' He smiled and Gillian relaxed. 'After all, we want to keep you in peak condition.'

'I suppose,' Gillian said reluctantly.

Katie could tell that the thought of anything interfering with her training was difficult for this young, driven woman. Then something struck her. 'Gillian, when you train, do you go running?'

'Yes. And go to the gym and do weights.'

'And when you go running, is it on a track? Or cross-country?'

'Across the fields near where I live. Why are you asking?'

Fabio and Katie exchanged a look. He nodded, inviting Katie to go on with her line of questioning.

'And these fields, is the grass long sometimes?'

'No,' Gillian replied. 'It would interfere with my running too much.' Her reply wasn't what Katie had hoped.

'But,' Gillian added, 'I do take a short cut home through the long grass as part of my cool-down.'

'Have you noticed a rash?' Fabio asked, and Katie knew he was thinking along the same lines she was.

'Come to think of it, I have. At least, my mother noticed it on my back. I didn't think anything of it. Do you think it's important?'

'It might be,' Katie said. It was just possible Gillian had been bitten by a tick and her symptoms had been caused by tick fever. In which case, it was good to catch it early and with the right treatment Gillian's sore joint would heal. To be certain, however, they would ask for Gillian's blood samples to be tested for the disease.

'I could give your knee some ultrasound treatment after Dr Lineham's taken some blood. That might well help. And I'll schedule you in for more when you come back to see the doctor for the results. How does that sound?'

Gillian nodded and quickly Fabio reached into the cupboards and pulled out a syringe and some vials for the blood.

'We should have the results tomorrow, if I rush them through,' he said, and after explaining what he was going to do slipped a needle into a vein in Gillian's arm.

'Okay, I'll get these over to the lab. Make sure you make an appointment to come back and see me the day after tomorrow. You can bring someone with you if you like.' He squeezed her shoulder. 'I know it's difficult and easy for me to say, but try not to worry.' With a last smile he left the room, taking the samples with him.

'He's kind of cute, isn't he?' Gillian said wistfully.

Katie smiled back. 'I can't say I noticed,' she lied. 'Come on, then, let's get some ultrasound on that knee.'

After Gillian had made another appointment and left, Katie went in search of Fabio. She knew the patient he had been waiting for had been and gone. She found him in the small kitchen drinking a glass of water.

'Thanks for seeing Gillian,' she said.

He held out a glass and raised an eyebrow. When she nodded he poured her a glass of water from the fridge.

'Never, ever think twice about seeking a medical opinion from one of us,' he said. 'Jonathan wasn't kidding when he said that we want our patients to get the best possible care and attention.'

Katie returned his look. 'Which is why I agreed to come and work for this practice,' she responded, her voice cool.

Fabio smiled sheepishly. 'Forgive me. I didn't

mean that to come out the way it did. We wouldn't have employed you if we hadn't been convinced you were the best fit for us. There are too many people who are willing to take money from patients for unnecessary treatment.'

'Do you think there's a chance she might have rheumatoid arthritis?' Katie asked, trying to ignore the way something in her stomach was performing little pirouettes every time he looked at her.

'I think it's possible, but it was a good call to check for Lyme disease. We can't be sure what it is until we've done all the tests and have the results back.'

'Poor Gillian. If she does have rheumatoid arthritis, this could mean the end of her dreams, couldn't it?'

'Let's not get ahead of ourselves, Katie.'

'But if...' she persisted.

His eyes were almost the colour of grass, Katie thought. Now, where had that come from? She had to remember that not only was Fabio her boss, and off limits for that reason on its own, but he was the kind of man who broke hearts. She had more than enough to deal with at the moment without developing a crush on her new colleague.

'If she does have arthritis then, yes, it won't be good for her career,' Fabio admitted. 'On the other hand, Lyme disease and a host of other possible conditions are easily treatable. And she will have you to thank for spotting it so early. But until we know what we're dealing with, I refuse to make any predictions. Rest assured, I'll do anything in my power so that she doesn't have to give up the sport she loves.' He pushed himself upright. 'Do you always worry so much about your patients?' he asked.

'I can't help it,' Katie admitted. 'These days I worry all the time, about everyone.'

He looked puzzled.

'Any particular reason it's *these days*?'

She was surprised he had picked up on her slip. Yet she felt this strange connection between them. The silence stretched between them as he studied her intently. 'Are you sure there's nothing you want to tell me?'

Katie shook her head. She didn't want to let him into her head any more than he was already.

'You can't go through life worrying about what

might happen. If you do, you'll end up missing what *is* happening,' Fabio continued softly.

He was right. Of course he was right. It was the same thing Suzy had said but that didn't mean she could change how she felt.

'I'll bear that in mind,' she said tightly. It was easy for him to say. Who did he care about?

Fabio gave her a sharp look but said nothing. He finished writing the labels for the bloods he had taken earlier and popped them in the tray to be collected for the lab. When he turned back to her the teasing look was back in his eyes.

'How do you fancy coming for a drink with me tonight? I have passes to the VIP area of Vipers.'

Katie's pulse thrummed. He was asking her out!

'I suspect you could do with some cheering up.' His eyes softened.

He was asking her out because he felt *sorry* for her? She wasn't going out with anyone just because they thought she needed cheering up. She had her pride after all. So much for thinking there was something between them. But neither, as she seemed to have to keep reminding herself, was she interested in him.

'I'm sorry, I can't.'

'Can't or won't, Katie?' He tilted her chin, forcing her to meet his eyes, and a flash of heat spiralled through her body.

She pulled away from him, needing to put distance between them. 'Won't. If you'll excuse me, I have a home visit to do.'

'Ah, yes,' Fabio replied. 'Lord Hilton. Actually, we're both going to see him. He had a stroke three weeks ago and you're scheduled to take over his daily physio. I need to check how he's doing. After that, we have a singer who was involved in a car accident a few weeks ago. She broke her arm, it's in a cast and I want to check and see how she's doing. She also needs some physio.'

'What sort of residual damage does Lord Hilton have?' Katie was glad to get the conversation back on neutral ground.

Fabio flicked a glance at his watch. 'He's expecting us in an hour. It will take us that long to get to his place. Why don't I bring you up to speed on the way?'

CHAPTER SIX

FABIO'S car was a surprise. Instead of the sports car she'd assumed he'd be driving, it was a perfectly respectable, solid family saloon. Fabio must have noticed her raised eyebrow. 'Not mine. It belongs to a friend. The one I usually drive is in the garage, undergoing repairs for a...er... scrape.'

Katie couldn't bring to herself to ask him what had happened. She wondered if Mark had known about the so-called scrape before he'd let Fabio anywhere near his racing car. The rueful look in Fabio's eyes made her smile. Whatever his faults, there was no denying there was something terribly attractive about him. No doubt most women found him irresistible.

As promised, Fabio launched into details of the patients they were going to see, while he weaved his way through the heavy London traffic.

'Lord Hilton is first on our list. Luckily he's

staying with his sister-in-law here in London while he recuperates, so we won't have to drive to his estate. His sister-in-law, Lady Hilton, is a big fan of the practice.'

'How bad was Lord Hilton's stroke?' Katie asked.

'It could have been worse. Apart from some residual weakness on his left side that makes it difficult for him to walk without help, he got off lightly. Unfortunately he has a fondness for cakes and pastries and no matter how often I tell him that he needs to reduce his cholesterol, he won't listen.' Fabio glanced at Katie through his thick, dark lashes. 'Perhaps he'll listen to you.'

'Me? I doubt that. If he's going to listen to anyone, surely it'll be you, his doctor.' And not just because he was his doctor. Katie was increasingly certain that Fabio could charm the birds out of the trees, young or old.

Fabio grinned. 'I might have been able to persuade him if it wasn't for the fact he's known me since I was in short trousers. My father's mother was his cousin. I think he still finds it difficult to accept that I'm old enough to be a doctor.'

Somehow Katie could simply not see Fabio as a

child. She was sure he must have sprung from his mother's womb beautifully dressed and immaculately mannered. The image made her giggle.

'What's funny?' Fabio asked as he swung the car down a broad street lined with Georgian townhouses.

'Nothing.' His glance told her that wouldn't do. 'Sorry. The image of you in a sleepsuit. I couldn't help myself. It's a little different to the way you are now.'

Fabio pretended to look offended, then smiled back. 'Any image of me that makes you laugh has to be good. I like to see you smile.'

Katie's pulse skipped a beat and for a moment the air between them was thick with something she couldn't quite put a finger on. Flustered, she turned her head away and stared out of the window.

Now, what had made him go and say that? Fabio chided himself. His teasing comments clearly made her uncomfortable, but he couldn't help it, no matter how often he told himself she was off limits. He wanted to see her smile. Since the evening in Monaco when he'd decided that sleeping with her was the only way to get her out of his system, he'd revised his plan. He couldn't bring himself to seduce her. Since meeting Katie, he wanted to believe that he was better than that. He wanted *her* to believe he was a better man than he was. For the umpteenth time, he found himself wondering what was causing the sadness that was always lurking, even when she smiled. Had someone hurt her? It made him want to grab whoever it was and shake him by the throat. Any fool could see that she was different from other women. She was shy and reserved and…honest. When Katie gave her heart, it would be without pretence or guile. Women like her deserved better.

Why was he tying himself in knots over her anyway? She was beautiful, not in the way other women were, her mouth was slightly too wide, her nose had a little bump that stopped it from being perfectly straight, and she had the tiniest gap between her two front teeth. For some reason, he found the whole package incredibly attractive. But it wasn't just that he found her sexy as hell, she had this unsettling effect on his psyche. She made him introspective, made him think about stuff that he had spent most of his life trying not thinking about. And—maybe this had more to do with his attraction than he wanted to admit—she seemed completely un-fazed by his attention. That in itself made her dif-ferent—and a challenge. He'd had his fair share of kiss-and-tells, some of the women whom he dated obviously finding the lure of who he was, or rather who his parents were, irresistible. One or two had even thought he would use his con-nections to kick-start their acting and singing careers. Those were the women who, once he'd steered them towards someone who might be able to help, he dropped like hotcakes. While he didn't mind non-serious relationships, indeed made it clear from the get-go that he wasn't into marriage and babies, neither did he like the feeling he was being used.

He slid a glance at his companion, who was staring out of the window. He was certain that she couldn't care less who his parents were or who he was connected to. Come to think of it, she didn't seem that impressed with him either. He hadn't intended to ask her out earlier, but some-how he had found himself doing exactly that.

And she'd said no! Her refusal had taken him by surprise. *Porra!* One way or another, he had to cure himself of his growing fixation with Katie Simpson before it got completely out of hand.

CHAPTER SEVEN

THE visit to Lord Hilton took longer than Katie had expected. The effects of his stroke had made him irritable and out of sorts. Thankfully Fabio had been able to cajole him into accepting the need for regular physio and once Katie had put him through a set of passive movements, Lord Hilton seemed to relax and was even grudgingly grateful.

Back in the car, Katie sighed. 'That was a bit uncom-fortable.'

Fabio smiled again. 'Don't worry about Lord H. His bark is worse than his bite. He liked you.'

'Liked me? I doubt that.'

'Trust me, he would have evicted you promptly if he hadn't been happy. He told me when you were washing your hands that you weren't too bad for someone of your age and that he supposed he'd be happy with you doing his physio. Believe me, that's praise coming from Hugh.'

It was all right for Fabio, Katie thought grumpily as they sped towards their next patient. He was clearly used to having people eating out of his hand.

Their next patient was a singer who had a car accident a number of weeks before. The singer, so famous even Katie had heard of her, was staying in one of London's leading hotels while she recovered.

'She has a house in London, as well as in New York and Los Angeles,' Fabio said, 'but she often stays in a hotel while she's touring in England.'

'Do you know her well?' Katie asked, trying not to show how starstruck she was.

'Not very,' Fabio said. 'She came to me with a medical problem the last time she was in London. Up until this accident she's been touring non-stop. In many ways it's not a bad thing her accident happened when it did. I warned her she had to slow down. People think it's all glamour, but the schedules some of these stars lead can be killers.'

'Was it like that for your father?' Katie asked.

A muscle twitched in Fabio's cheek and he frowned.

'I wouldn't know. Between my father's career and my mother's, I didn't see that much of them.' Although his voice was light, Katie thought she saw a shadow cross his face, but before she could be sure, it was gone. 'On the other hand, whenever I was with them life was always exciting.'

And Katie knew how much Fabio craved excitement. However, she wasn't convinced by his glib response.

'But as a child? What was it like for you?' she persisted. 'What about school and friends? Did you travel with your parents?'

Fabio steered the car though the heavy traffic before replying.

'I travelled with them on and off until it was time for me to go to school. Then I went to boarding school, along with several others who had parents in show business. Jonathan was there too. It's how we met. I spent some school holidays with my folks. Mostly in Brazil. Sometimes in London.' As a life story it was short and to the point. Clearly Fabio didn't like talking about his past.

'Do you go to Brazil to see your mother?' Katie

persisted. His reluctance to share the details of his life made her even more curious.

Once again Fabio paused. 'I haven't seen her for years. We don't really have much to say to each other.' He drummed his fingers on the steering-wheel. 'Maybe it's time I did something about that.' He sounded surprised, as if the thought hadn't crossed his mind before.

Katie wanted to probe deeper, but before she could they pulled up in front of the hotel and a doorman rushed to open the car door for them.

'I'll get someone to park your car for you, sir,' the doorman offered. Fabio tossed him the keys and led Katie into the hotel.

'Tamsin has a suite on the top floor,' Fabio told Katie.

Her head swivelled as she caught sight of various famous faces in the lobby, some of whom waved at Fabio as they passed by. She even thought she saw a minor royal sipping coffee. It was all head-spinning stuff. Like being in a dream. She only wished she were. Then Richard would still be alive and everything would be as it should be.

As the lift glided up to the top floor Katie

was acutely aware of Fabio. He confused her. When she'd first met him, she'd thought she'd dislike him. He'd appeared to be the epitome of a playboy, but she was beginning to realise that there was far more to this man than his gorgeous looks. He was kind and thoughtful and sympathetic. No wonder his patients, even grouchy Lord Hilton, seemed to adore him. But how much was a facade? What was underneath?

'You should be aware, if you don't already know, that Tamsin is going through a messy divorce at the moment. She's pretty cut up about it,' Fabio said.

It seemed that celebrity status and wealth was no barrier to pain.

Tamsin opened the door to them and invited them in.

Katie had never been in a hotel room like it before. In fact, it wasn't a room but a suite with breathtaking views of the Thames and London Bridge.

'Fabio, thanks so much for coming here,' Tamsin said with a genuine smile of gratitude. 'I couldn't face running the gauntlet of the paparazzi at the moment. They wait for me everywhere.'

Katie felt a stab of sympathy. It must be horrible enough to be going through a divorce without having all the details spelled out in the papers for everyone to read.

'This is Katie, our physio, Tamsin,' Fabio introduced her. 'She's going to have a look at your shoulder and leave you some exercises to do.'

Tamsin smiled again. 'I can't afford to have my shoulder seize up,' she said. 'It's the one I hold the microphone with. I'm due to sing at a concert in a couple of weeks.'

'There's no reason why you shouldn't have full use of your arm once the cast comes off,' Katie reassured her. 'The exercises will help you regain full mobility that much quicker, that's all.'

'How have you been, Tamsin?' Fabio asked. 'Are you getting some rest?'

Tamsin shrugged. 'I could do with some sleeping pills if you have any in that magic bag of yours. I had to cancel some venues but my sponsors have slotted in some extra dates to make up for the ones I've missed. I really need to be at my best if I'm gong to cope.'

Fabio's expression darkened and he shook his head. 'I'm sorry. I don't think sleeping pills are a good idea. Perhaps if you could get some exercise, that would help you sleep.'

Tamsin pouted. 'Are you sure you can't give me some? I can't even leave the hotel to see you, let alone to exercise. My personal trainer comes here, but there isn't much I can do. Not with my arm in a cast. Go on, Fabio, be a sweetie.'

But Fabio shook his head again. His mouth was set in a grim line. 'I can't stop you going to another doctor who will give you sleeping tablets, but I'm afraid I won't. It's too easy to become dependent on them.'

Tamsin sighed. 'I don't want another doctor, Fabio. I trust you.'

Fabio checked Tamsin's shoulder as well as taking some blood. 'I want to make sure there isn't another reason for your tiredness apart from a too-hectic schedule,' he explained. When he'd finished, Katie put Tamsin through some passive movements.

'When does the plaster come off?' Katie asked.

'A week tomorrow, thank God. You have no idea how difficult it is to bath and dress while keeping a cast dry. And,' she added, 'it is not a good look with an evening dress. Which reminds me...' She eyed Fabio hopefully. 'I have tickets for Vipers tonight. Everybody is going to be there. I hear that waste of space who used to be my husband is going with his latest fancy. I don't suppose you'd be willing to accompany a woman in an evening dress and arm cast, would you?'

'Sorry, Tamsin, but you know the rules. You're my patient.'

Tamsin pouted but clearly realised Fabio wouldn't change his mind. 'I could always change my doctor,' she said teasingly.

Fabio smiled coolly. 'Still wouldn't be allowed, Tamsin. Sorry.'

Katie hid a smile. At least there were some rules Fabio wasn't prepared to break.

'So what do you think of Tamsin?' Fabio asked as they waited for his car to be brought round to the front of the hotel. 'Is she like you imagined?'

'Not at all,' Katie admitted. 'The newspapers make her out to be some kind of monster, but I liked her.'

'The newspapers are wrong about a lot.' Fabio's lips thinned. 'I've been on the receiving end of their fabrications more than once.'

He tipped the doorman and opened the car door for her.

'You'll find that the patients we deal with, although often rich and famous, are, under the surface, like most people. Perhaps a little more insecure than most.' He smiled at her. 'More insecure than you, at any rate. You have a natural way with them. It's good that you don't let their celebrity status get in the way of how you treat them. It would be easy to be bullied into doing what they want rather than what's right for them.'

'Like Tamsin and the sleeping pills?'

'Exactly. There are plenty of unscrupulous doctors out there who are prepared to give those rich enough or famous enough anything they ask for. Even if it ends up killing them.' The bleak look she thought she'd seen earlier was back. It made Katie wonder how much of the rumours and speculation surrounding his father's death were true. The papers had reported his death as being the result of an accidental overdose. In that case, no wonder Fabio had taken a firm line with Tamsin.

'But they trust you.'

'It helps that I'm part of their world. They know I'd rather lose them as a patient than compromise my ethics. And if they don't…' he shrugged '…they can go elsewhere.'

She believed him. Underneath his light-hearted demeanour ran a thread of steel. It would have been better had he not been someone she could admire. Far, far easier to resist the magnetism that radiated from his every pore.

'That's us finished for the day. How about I run you home?' Fabio suggested.

'Oh, there's no need. Just drop me at the tube station.'

Again that dazzling smile. 'It's no problem. You've had a busy day and at this time the tube is packed.'

'Don't tell me you know from first-hand experience. I won't believe you.'

He pulled a face. 'No, you're right. The last time I used the tube was years ago and nothing would tempt me to use it again. It takes far too long, apart from anything else.'

'In which case, a lift home would be very nice.'

'Are you sure you won't change your mind about tonight?'

'So you can cheer me up?' She couldn't keep the asperity from her voice.

He looked at her in surprise. 'Because I like being with you,' he said softly.

The world seemed to shrink until it contained only them. Katie's heart tumbled in her chest. She didn't know how to behave, what to do with this man. Every instinct was screaming to keep their relationship professional while another part of her wanted nothing more than to be with him.

She forced herself to listen to her brain. Much more sensible.

'I can't, really.' She smiled. 'But thanks for asking.'

He looked at her, the expression in his green eyes unreadable. After what seemed like minutes, but could have only been seconds, he bent over and touched her cheek with his lips.

'Goodbye, Katie. I'll see you on Monday. Have a good weekend.' Then, with a casual wave of his hand, he was gone.

Katie touched her cheek with her fingertips.

Every minute she was becoming more confused by him. Did he really want to spend time with her, or was he just being friendly to a colleague he knew was going through a bad time? And why did it matter?

The next morning Fabio was up and out before it was light. He'd spent the night tossing and turning, trying not to think of Katie. It hadn't worked. He kept thinking about the way he felt when he was with her. Peaceful was the word that sprang to mind and since when did he do peaceful? On the other hand, the way she kept probing into his life, while studying him with those steady grey eyes, unsettled him. Already he had shared more with her about his life than he had with any other woman. And no matter how often he told himself that she was off limits, he kept looking for opportunities to be alone with her. It was as if his head and his heart belonged to two different people.

At dawn he'd given up on trying to get back to sleep and after dressing quickly had jumped into his car. Driving at speed, he had reached the cliffs just as it was getting light.

He checked the buckles of his parachute once more. Everything was secure. It had to be. In this sport, nothing could be left to chance. It was risky enough as it was.

He walked across to the side of the cliff and studied the contours of the mountain one final time.

There was plenty of clearance as long as he jumped away from the cliff and turned the right way. He would open his parachute about half-way down. Adrenaline rushed through his body, almost making him giddy. He loved the feeling. He never felt more alive than when he was jumping or surfing one of the big waves.

Although he wasn't his father, perhaps they were more alike than he wanted to admit. Dad had needed constant excitement in his life in ever-increasing amounts and he himself did too. But he chose to get his thrills from testing himself against the elements—unlike his father who had found his escape in drink and drugs until eventually they had killed him. Far better to die doing something like this than by drinking yourself into an early grave. At least *he* had no child, neither would he ever have one, to worry about leaving behind. No woman either. Or none that were ever likely to be a permanent feature. They were a necessary and enjoyable part of his life, but as soon as they got too serious he broke it off—he didn't want or need emotional entanglement. He didn't want to be responsible for another human being and especially not their happiness. Why then did he have to keep reminding himself of that these days?

All he could remember from the time his parents were still together was raised voices, slamming doors and then his father staring into the fire with a drink in his hand. They'd been exciting but indifferent parents. He missed the excitement, but as for the indifference, he'd learned from early on only to rely on himself. That way no one got hurt.

Recently he had started wondering if he was drawn to extreme sports because something was missing in his life.

Fabio knew he and the other small select band of BASE jumpers were alike underneath. They were all always looking for the next challenge, taking ever-increasing risks, needing bigger and bigger thrills. Sometimes these risks paid off and new records were broken; sometimes they didn't and people died. It was an acceptable part of their sport. Although the authorities never saw it that way. They were always trying to limit access for the jumpers. Not that Fabio really wanted to jump off buildings. He preferred being out in the open, away from the city.

He took one last deep breath and flung himself into the air. God! There was no feeling in the world that could ever replace what he felt at this moment.

CHAPTER EIGHT

'HEY, anyone seen the latest photo of our Fabulous Fabio?' Jenny plonked the tabloid newspaper down in the staff kitchen where they were all gathered, with the exception of Fabio who hadn't yet arrived, to discuss the day's patients.

Jonathan picked it up and grinned. 'What's he been up to this time?' He let out a low whistle. 'That's some stunner he's with. He didn't tell me he has a new woman.'

'Not that you could keep track, darling, even if he did. We both know Fabio changes his girlfriends the way other people change their socks,' Rose said with a mischievous smile. 'I'm just glad the paparazzi aren't so interested in you these days.'

Jonathan wrapped his arms around his wife's shoulders. 'Not very playboy to have a heavily pregnant wife, is it? *Oof.* What did you do that for?' he grunted as his wife elbowed him in the stomach. 'You know which one I'd rather have on my arm any day of the week.'

Katie sneaked a look at the newspaper. Her heart thudded uncomfortably against her ribs when she saw that the picture was of Fabio and the co-pilot they'd met on their trip to Monaco. He had an arm around her narrow waist as she leaned against him. Almost matched in height, the blonde still managed to look as if she was gazing up at Fabio adoringly. And as for him, he was grinning down at her as if he couldn't tear his eyes away.

She felt disappointed and hurt and angry. It wasn't as if Fabio and herself were anything more than colleagues. Why then did she want to tear the paper into tiny little shreds? Now she knew for certain why he had asked her out. Out of sympathy—that was all. He'd probably been re-lieved when she'd said no so he could take Miss Drop-Dead Gorgeous. She should have trusted her instincts. Fabio Lineham was not a man to rely on and the photograph was a timely reminder of that.

'She's gorgeous,' Jenny was saying. 'Does anyone know who she is? I don't recognise her.'

'She's a pilot,' Katie said, and blushed as curious eyes turned to look at her. 'She was the co-pilot on the trip we made to Monaco.'

Jonathan laughed. 'Trust Fabio never to miss an opportunity to get himself a date with a beautiful... *Oof*,' he gasped as Rose elbowed him again. 'I mean a horrible, not-my-type-at-all woman.'

Vicki was also studying the photograph. 'I think she's got a mean look to her, if you ask me,' she said. 'Why can't Fabio find a woman who he can fall in love with? He can't go on playing the field for ever.'

'Who can't?' Fabio asked as he came into the room. He took the newspaper from Vicki and tossed it on the coffee table. 'You guys, of all people, should know not to believe everything you see in the papers.'

'So, you're telling us the picture is made up?' Vicki teased. 'Too bad we all know you too well.'

'Anyway, back to work,' Rose said. 'I thought I should tell you that as we've agreed, we're advertising for some more staff. A paediatrician to take over some of the children and an obstetrician and gynaecologist. More and more of our ante-natal patients are wanting the practice to see them all the way through labour and beyond.'

'And a new nurse?' Vicki said hopefully. 'It's not long until you go on maternity leave, Rose, and we have more than enough patients as it is.'

'That too.' Rose smiled and pressed a hand to her belly. 'I think he just kicked me!'

As the rest of the staff, with the exception of Fabio, crowded around the expectant mother, Katie slipped outside into the reception area.

'You okay?' She whirled round to find Fabio standing behind her, studying her quizzically.

'Sure. Why shouldn't I be?' Just because I thought you cared just a little for me—she thought the words, knowing that she would never say them.

Fabio looked as if he was about to say something, but just then the bell on the door rang, announcing their next patient, and Jenny rushed into the room.

'Cripes,' she said. 'I almost forgot. Sheikh Mustaf is bringing his two children to see you, Fabio. It's a first visit, so we'd better not keep him.'

Later, after Katie had seen the three patients

scheduled for treatment, including Gillian, who did turn out to have Lyme disease and whose stiff limbs were improving. Just as Gillian left, Fabio popped his head around the door.

'I have two tickets for a film premiere next week and I'm looking for company. My cousin Kendrick is in it and I promised him I'd go.'

'What about Drop-Dead Gorgeous?' Katie muttered under her breath.

'Who? What did you say?' Fabio looked perplexed as he walked towards her. Katie stared. There was something wrong with the way he was moving. Yes, he was decidedly favouring his left leg.

'What's wrong with your leg?' Katie asked, her chagrin with him momentarily forgotten.

'Nothing much. Now, what were you saying? Something about dropping dead? I hope that wasn't directed at me?'

'Sit down on my couch and either roll up your trouser leg or take your trousers off,' Katie said firmly.

'You want me to undress?' Fabio's eyes gleamed. 'Are you sure this is the time or the place?'

Katie gave him a none-too-gentle shove. 'Sit,' she said. 'Can't you do as you're told for once?'

Something in her expression must have warned him she was in no mood for joking around. He sat on the couch and rolled up his left trouser leg. 'See? Nothing wrong.'

'The other one, please, Fabio.'

Reluctantly he did as she asked. Katie bent and studied his ankle. It was swollen and badly bruised.

'When and how did you do this?'

'On Saturday,' Fabio conceded. 'But it's nothing. You should see—' He broke off.

'See…?' When he remained stubbornly silent she asked him again. 'What happened?'

'I was jumping at the weekend and let's just say there was a rock where the ground should have been flat.'

'You should be more careful,' Katie said tightly.

Fabio shrugged. 'What's the fun in being careful? Ouch! That hurt.'

Katie was unaware that she was squeezing Fabio's injured ankle, but she gave it another squeeze for good measure. It was only a sprain but, knowing Fabio and his recklessness, it could just as easily have been broken.

She stood up abruptly. 'Ice is what you need for that ankle. But you know that.'

'Hey, what did I say?' Fabio looked genuinely baffled. 'You're mad at me. Why?'

'You shouldn't be doing stuff that might stop you from working. You have a responsibility to keep yourself fit. How else are you going to look after your patients?'

'I don't take unnecessary risks, believe me.' He studied her through half-closed eyes and a slow smile spread across his face. 'Don't tell me you're worried about me.'

'Of course I'm not.' Katie turned away so he couldn't read her expression. She was angry with him, but whether it was because of the photo in the paper or the fact he didn't seem to care what he did with himself, she didn't know.

Fabio hopped off the examination couch, grimacing as he put weight on his ankle. Katie felt his hand on her shoulder and he whirled her round so she was forced to look into his eyes.

'*Te, te, te, minha linda*, don't care about me too much.'

And then he dropped his hand and, leaving her speechless, left the room.

The days settled into a rhythm. In the mornings they would meet over coffee and discuss the patients who were expected in for treatment as well as those requiring home visits.

Katie was kept so busy it hardly gave her time to think. When she wasn't seeing patients at the clinic, she was either out seeing patients in their homes on her own or with Fabio or another doctor at the clinic. Little Lucy was doing well and Katie often went to their house to carry out her physio.

One day Fabio sought her out.

'I have a couple of tickets for that movie premiere and I wondered if you'd changed your mind about coming with me. My cousin is in it. He'll probably be there as he's between movies at the moment.'

'Your cousin is a movie star?'

Fabio grinned. 'Kendrick's not exactly a film star. Although he could have been.'

'I'm confused.'

'He's the stuntman. If you think I like risking my neck, I can assure you I have nothing on Kendrick. I don't think he's happy unless he risks it at least once a day.'

Then the memory of the film star on the yacht talking about Kendrick came back to her. Kendrick was the cousin who'd been in the army before becoming a stuntman. She shuddered. 'What is it about some men that they can't be happy unless they're behaving like Rambo? I feel sorry for his wife.'

'Kendrick hasn't got a wife. Not the marrying kind, I guess. Doesn't seem to run in our family for some reason.'

It was another subtle reminder—as if she needed one—that whatever this was that was between them, it wasn't to be taken seriously.

'I'm sure you'll find someone else to take easily enough,' she said stiffly.

'I'd like to take *you*.' A smile played on his lips. 'I promise you I'll be a perfect gentleman. You'll be perfectly safe with me. Just two colleagues having an evening out together.'

Katie tried to ignore the disappointment she felt at his words. Hadn't she decided that she and Fabio had very little in common?

'Please,' he said again. 'I really would enjoy

your company tonight. I can relax when I'm with you. Unless, of course…' his smile widened '…you don't feel that you can trust yourself with me.'

He really was the most arrogant man.

'Don't be ridiculous,' Katie retorted, stung. 'I wouldn't fall for you if you were the last man on earth—whatever misapprehension you're labouring under.'

That told him. But it made her sound about three years old. His eyes had widened with surprise and was it something else? Satisfaction? Damn. Even to her own ears her protestation sounded remarkably like a case of the lady protesting too much.

'I'm sorry,' she added hastily. 'I don't know where that came from. It was rude and unnecessary. Of course I'd love to go.' Now, that was better. That was the normal response to a colleague who was being friendly. It wasn't as if they'd be alone. Surrounded by people, he wouldn't be able to tempt her with his dark green eyes and dangerously sexy mouth. And if her heart bumped against her ribs, it was nothing to do with wanting to spend time with Fabio. Nothing at all.

* * *

Katie was nervous as she dressed for her date. Not that it was a date, she reminded herself. He needed a companion for the evening, that was all.

Suzy had put Ricky down for the night and was perched on the edge of Katie's bed with a mug of cocoa.

'Now, you have to note everything,' Suzy said. 'I want to know it all. Who was there, what they were wearing. *Especially* what they are wearing.'

Before Suzy had gone on maternity leave she had been a buyer for one of the more upmarket fashion chains. She had always been bringing home clothes and up until her pregnancy and Richard's death had been one of those women who looked stunning whatever they wore. Suzy had loved Katie's descriptions of the people at the party on the yacht and waited eagerly every evening to hear about the women who came to the clinic.

'I don't know, Suzy. I think I should phone him and tell him I can't go. I don't want to leave you on your own and, besides, the thought of being in the company of all those beautiful people terrifies me.'

'Don't be ridiculous,' Suzy said firmly. 'You

can outshine them anytime. As for me…' she reached over and touched Katie on the hand '…I'm doing okay. It's you I'm worried about.'

When Katie went to protest, Suzy cut her off.

'I know you feel the pain of Richard's death as much as I do. I'm trying to look to the future, even though the fact it doesn't include Richard hurts like crazy. I know in some ways it's worse for you. At least I have Ricky and my parents, but Richard was the only family you had left. I made a promise to him, remember? Part of that promise is pushing you to get on with your life too. So think of tonight as you doing it for me, okay?'

A lump in her throat, Katie reached over and the two women hugged briefly.

'Okay. For you. And because Richard would never forgive me if I didn't,' Katie said. 'Now, what *am* I going to wear?'

Suzy had insisted that they go shopping for something new for Katie to wear to the premiere. It had taken longer than any other shopping expedition Katie could remember, but Suzy wouldn't give up until they'd found the perfect dress. It was an off-the-shoulder, two-tone, silky, floor-length evening dress in blood red. Not something Katie would have ever chosen for herself, but she had to admit it made her feel sexy and sophisticated.

Fabio collected her, and when she came down the stairs, he whistled under his breath.

'*Deus*, you look stunning,' he said simply.

'You don't look too bad yourself.' Katie smiled back. He was wearing a dinner jacket and a crisp white shirt open at the neck.Five o'clock stubble shadowed his chin, if anything making him look more dangerously sexy than before.

Katie noticed that Fabio was driving a sports car. He must have retrieved it from the panel beater. At least in London he couldn't drive as if he were on a racing track. He opened the door with a flourish and, feeling a bit like Cinderella, Katie slid into the soft leather seat.

'I wondered if you'd change your mind,' he said as they pulled away.

'I did think about it, but here I am.'

Fabio slid her a glance. 'I'm very glad you are.' The smile he gave her made her heart hum and she was thankful that the darkness hid the heat that rose to her face.

Although Katie had seen clips of film premieres on television, the experience of actually being there was something else entirely. She doubted whether she had ever seen so many photographers in one place before.

It was impossible to ignore the cameras, seeing as the minute they stepped out of the car flashbulbs popped and dazzled like a million exploding stars as the photographers pointed their cameras at them.

'Fabio! Look this way! Who's the lady? What is your mother up to? Does she have another film lined up?'

Fixing a smile on his face, Fabio gripped Katie by the elbow and steered her along the red carpet.

'Just look straight ahead and try to smile,' he whispered in her ear. 'They'll soon turn their attention to someone else. There are plenty bigger fish here tonight than me.'

It was easy for him. He didn't have to worry about getting four-inch heels stuck in the hem of an evening dress that had cost Katie almost a month's salary, only to have the picture appear in a newspaper. She smothered a giggle. Who would have thought only a couple of weeks ago that she'd be worried about having her picture in a newspaper?

'Pretend they're all naked—it works for me,' Fabio whispered in her ear, making her laugh, and she relaxed. It was surreal, being here, being photographed alongside the rich and famous. It would be another memory to stash away for her grandchildren.

Nevertheless, by the time they were safely inside, away from the photographers' lenses, she found herself sympathising with those in the public eye. Although she knew that many sought publicity, it couldn't be easy to be constantly under scrutiny. Was that what it had been like for Fabio when growing up? No wonder he seemed so self-assured.

Just then a tall, muscular man in his early thirties approached them and flung his arm around Fabio's shoulder.

'Fabio, good you could make it.' Piercing blue eyes turned on Katie and the man gave her an appreciative look. 'And who's this?'

'Hands off, Kendrick. She's with me,' Fabio growled. 'Katie, I'd like you to meet my cousin, Kendrick. Kendrick, this is Katie.'

'Pleased to meet you, ma'am.' The accent was mildly American and the voice held an undercurrent of amusement. Kendrick grinned at Katie. 'Any time you get tired of going out with this Pom, I'd be glad to show you around.'

Another flirt. Did every man in Fabio's family behave the same way?

'You must be the stuntman,' Katie said. 'I'm really looking forward to seeing your film.'

'You won't even see me,' Kendrick warned. 'It's my job to make it look as if the hero is doing it all himself. I wouldn't have come to London to see it except I happen to have heard there's some good waves in Ireland this weekend.' He turned to Fabio. 'Are you up for it?'

Fabio grinned. 'Count me in.'

'You surf too?' Katie asked.

Kendrick flicked his eyes at Fabio. 'I guess some people would call it surfing. Others call it Big Wave. Regular surfing is for ladies.'

What was that supposed to mean?

'I've got a 'copter lined up and a couple of jet skis,' Kendrick continued. 'So we're sorted.' He looked at his watch. 'If you'll excuse me, the film is about to start and my date is waiting.' He nodded across to a film star with a metallic dress who, although surrounded by adoring men, kept looking Kendrick's way.

'It was good to meet you, Katie. I hope to see you again.' There was no mistaking the speculative look in Kendrick's eye as he glanced at Fabio. 'Something tells me I'm going to.' And with that he threaded his way back into the crowd.

'What does he mean, some people call it crazy? What kind of surfing needs a jet ski and a helicopter?' Katie asked Fabio.

'Pay no attention to Kendrick,' Fabio said evasively. 'Let's go and take our seats.'

As soon as the film started, Katie knew she had made a dreadful mistake. Why hadn't she thought to look it up? The title, *One Saturday in December*, hadn't given any indication that it was a movie about war. She gripped the edge of her seat as images spooled in front of her. Men under fire. Men being shot. Men flying in the air as bombs exploded all around them. She felt sick. Was that how it had been for Richard? The noise, the flying dirt, the relentless fear? Had he been terrified in those last few minutes of his life? Had he been in pain? Calling out for Suzy?

Knowing he would never see Ricky or any of his family again? Katie's heart felt as if it was shattering into tiny pieces.

Unable to bear one more minute, she knew she had to get out of there.

'Excuse me,' she whispered to Fabio. 'I have to get past. I need to go.'

Immediately he was on his feet. Ignoring the impatient sighs of the audience, she shuffled up the row. Her hands were clammy and she felt physically sick. She stumbled outside, taking deep breaths of fresh air, trying to get herself back under control.

'What is it?' Fabio was by her side, his steadying hand on her elbow.

She couldn't speak. She could barely breathe. She had to get away, find some corner where she could be alone.

Fabio hailed a passing taxi and ushered her inside. 'I'm taking you home.' Long fingers felt her pulse. 'Your pulse is racing,' he said.

'Not home,' she whispered. She couldn't let Suzy see her like this. She couldn't face her until she got herself under control. Suzy needed her to be strong. Not this falling-apart wreck she was right now.

She was aware of cool fingers on her over-heated skin as he touched her forehead.

'A bit clammy. A touch of flu maybe.' He frowned. 'At least, that's what I would think if you hadn't been okay before the film started.'

'It's not flu,' Katie said miserably.

'Driver, take us to Tower Bridge,' Fabio told the driver.

She was grateful for his silence as the taxi drove towards the river. Katie wanted to be outside. She needed fresh air and the darkness.

By the time the taxi dropped them she knew where she wanted to go. Somewhere she went almost every week since she'd come back to London. On the Thames Riverbus, going up the river and returning without getting off, surrounded by strangers, was the one place she could be alone with her thoughts and memories.

'You can go back to the movie,' she said to Fabio. 'I'm going to take the riverbus. I'll be fine, I promise you. I just need to be alone. Or at least not with anyone I know.'

'If you think I'm going to let you go anywhere

by yourself, you're crazy.' His mouth tipped up at one corner. 'Anyway, I've never been on the riverbus.'

Katie didn't have the strength to argue with him; besides, she knew she'd be only wasting her time.

They found a seat right at the back where they could be on their own. The tourists were happy to get the best seats near the front. As they passed the Parliament buildings, Fabio leaned back and placed his arms behind his head.

'This is cool. Why have I never thought of doing this before?'

'Because it's not your style?'

'Hey, how do you know what my style is?'

He was right. She still knew very little about him, even if she felt as if they were connected by a gossamer-fine thread.

He said nothing as the boat continued upriver. She knew she owed him an explanation for her behaviour, otherwise he was going to think his colleague was seriously kooky. But what could she say?

Right now she was grateful for his silence.

Eventually he spoke.

'I can tell you're hurting. *Porra!* A blind man could see it. I think you should tell me.'

The darkness of the night, the sympathy in his voice, this connection she felt with him, whatever it was, at last she knew she was ready to tell him.

'On the plane to Monaco I told you I didn't have any brothers or sisters. It wasn't the truth. I had a brother. A much-loved brother. He died a few months ago.' Her voice caught on the words. It was still so difficult to say. So difficult to believe. 'He was a doctor in Afghanistan.'

His hand covered hers and she was grateful for its warmth. 'It still hurts. When our parents died, it was only me and him. Kind of the two of us against the world. We had no one else to depend on, so we relied on each other. He was older than me, eighteen to my thirteen. Somehow, I don't know how, he persuaded the authorities that I shouldn't go into care. That he would look after me. He was about to start med school. He gave up any social life he might have had so he could be there when I came home from school. He was the one who told me about boys,' She attempted a smile. 'Not that it did me much good.' She swallowed the lump in her throat. 'He was the one who was there when I went through puberty, the one who comforted me when I wanted my mum, the one who dried my tears when my first boyfriend dumped me. He was there. He was always there.'

Fabio's arm came around her shoulder and as she leaned into him it felt the most natural thing in the world.

'Our parents left us the house so we had somewhere to stay, but money was tight. When I told Richard that I wanted to be a physio, he agreed to let the army put him through medical school in return for staying with them after he'd graduated.'

Fabio pulled her closer. She closed her eyes, remembering. 'He said he didn't mind. He loved being a doctor—he was an A and E specialist, and he knew he was playing his part, helping the troops. He always claimed it didn't matter whether you believed in war or not, the soldiers deserved the best medical care the country had to offer. And he was one of the best.'

She could feel Fabio's heart beating through the thin material of his shirt.

'That's what Kendrick believes too,' Fabio said.

'He hated the fact of war but always said some-one had to do it. He was a career soldier, though. He knew the risks. Unlike your brother.'

It was too dark for Katie to read his expression as she continued.

'It wasn't just the funding that attracted him to the life. He loved it that he could spend his weekends outdoors learning new sports. I still remember how excited he was about his first jump from a plane.'

They were both silent for a while as Katie struggled to find the words. 'Before he went to Afghanistan for the first time, he met the woman who was to become his wife. My sister-in-law, Suzy. He was so happy. He promised he'd do a couple of tours and come home. Then, just before his second tour, Suzy told him she was pregnant. He was so excited. We both were. He was going to have his own family, one that he made very clear I'd always be part of. I was going to be an aunty, my brother had found the perfect woman, I had qualified as a physio. Life was good. We never really thought about the possibility he'd be called up to work in a war zone, never mind have to go where the fighting was the fiercest. But of course they need doctors as close to the soldiers as possible. Not that Richard told us that he was expected to go there. He let us believe that he was safely in at base camp. I don't know if you know it, but it's well protected and the medical staff there are believed to be pretty safe.'

Her throat was so tight she could barely speak.

Fabio squeezed her hand and waited silently for her to continue.

'What we didn't know was that Richard had to do a stint at one of the forward operating bases. That's in enemy-held territory. You know, with the troops as they go on patrol. It's a job for doctors who are soldiers too.'

'So I've heard,' Fabio said.

'Knowing Richard, they wouldn't even have had to ask him. He would have felt it was his duty to go. If soldiers in his regiment were putting their lives at risk, he would have wanted to be there to help them if they needed it.'

Her voice was shaky and she turned away from Fabio, trying to hide the tremble in her hands.

'To cut a long story short, he was with them when they came under attack. Richard could have stayed safe until it was all over, but, no—'

she couldn't keep the bitterness from creeping in '—he had to go out under fire to pull an injured soldier to safety. Not once, but twice. It was on the second occasion that he got shot. The only good thing is that it was instantaneous, or so they say...'

'They wouldn't lie to you about that.' Fabio pulled her more firmly into the crook of his arm. 'If they say it was instant, you should believe them.'

Katie tasted the salt of her tears. She hadn't even realised she was crying.

'The two soldiers he went to save are going to be okay. One had to have a leg amputated and the other was in hospital for a few months, but they say he's going to be fine, so at least Richard didn't die for nothing. We find some comfort in that.'

'So you're all alone. Parents dead and now your only brother.' He let out a low whistle. 'My poor girl. It's not fair. How old are you? Twenty-four?'

'Twenty-six.' She managed a smile. 'I'm older than I look. Life isn't fair,' she added quietly. 'I don't know why we think it should be. Richard wasn't the only person to be killed that day. There were four others who died along with him. Four other families going through the pain of losing someone. Fathers, mothers, sisters, brothers, children.' Her voice hitched and she drew a shaky breath. 'At least he died doing something he loved and there was some purpose to his death. I try to take some comfort from that.'

Fabio took his arm from her shoulder and turned her so she was facing him. He took a clean handkerchief from his pocket and gently dabbed the tears away.

'He must make you very proud,' he said finally when he'd finished.

'He does. But that doesn't make up for the way I feel. Right now, I would give anything to have him back. Anything. And I'm sure the families of the other men who died that day feel the same. As for Suzy—all her dreams are shattered. Instead of bringing up Ricky with Richard, she's going to have to do it on her own. How can any of that be right?' She sniffed loudly and took his handkerchief from his hand and blew loudly. 'What I find difficult to understand is how Amelia can watch Mark race and not be terrified. What if he's killed? She'll be just like Suzy. Left with a child to bring up on her own. It's even worse for her, knowing that she could lose Lucy too. I could never, ever do what she does. Especially not now. One thing is for sure, I will never, ever marry a man who puts himself in danger. I won't go through what Suzy did and what Amelia does. I'm not strong enough.'

'I think you're stronger than you think, Katie. You'll feel differently in time. The pain will go, I promise. Not completely, I'm told it never does that, but it will get better.'

Suddenly conscious that she was holding his sodden hanky in her hands, Katie was horrified. It was completely inappropriate, never mind un-professional, to break down in the arms of her colleague, no matter how kind and sympathetic he'd been. She pulled away from his embrace and stepped away.

'I'm sorry. I don't know what you must think. Someone you hardly know, and a colleague to boot, crying all over you.' She dabbed ineffectu-ally at the front of his damp white shirt with his hanky and steadied her breathing. 'I can assure you, if you can believe me, that it's not something I usually do.'

'Don't worry about it. I'm kind of used to women crying,' he said.

She stepped away. Of all the insufferable comments. Trying to make out he was used to women breaking their hearts over him. Just as she was beginning to think she'd misjudged him all along.

'I bet you are,' she said stiffly.

His eyes were amused. 'I'm talking about patients,' he said. 'What did you think I meant?'

She was always misreading him. After he'd been kind.

'I think I'm ready to go home now,' she said.

Fabio dropped Katie at her sister-in-law's house and sent the taxi away. He would walk the five miles to his flat. It had taken all his willpower back on the riverbus not to take Katie in his arms and kiss the tears away. Instinctively he'd known it wasn't the time. When he kissed her for the first time, he didn't want it to be because she was vulnerable.

Deus. How many times did he have to remind himself that kissing Katie would lead to a relationship, which would lead to trouble? He forced the image of her mouth out of his head.

No wonder Katie was guarded. The loss of her brother explained a lot.

At least Richard had died for something he'd believed in. What did *he* believe in? Nothing. Only living life to the full. The next thrill. The here and now—his sport. Certainly not the future. He didn't want happy families. Not that he believed happy families truly existed—even if Katie seemed to think her brother's marriage was different. His parents had torn each other apart even before his father had become dependent on drugs. At least at boarding school he hadn't had to witness his parents fighting. He remembered hiding in a cupboard once, terrified that his parents' arguing was about him and that if he disappeared, perhaps they would be happy. At boarding school he'd been lonely at first. He'd thought his parents had sent him away because they didn't love him. It had hurt, but if it meant the arguments would stop, it was worth the empty feeling inside he had for most of his childhood. But his parents had divorced anyway and no one had come to fetch him back from school. It had taught him one thing. To rely on himself. Not to count on anyone else for happiness.

Fabio let himself into his flat, flinging his car keys onto the coffee table where they landed with a clatter. It was so quiet in here. Why had he never noticed?

Ignoring the red light on his phone that indicated that there were messages waiting for him, he went into the kitchen and poured himself a fruit juice. He never drank alcohol. With his father, he had seen first hand what a reliance on chemical stimulants could do to a person. Not that he was at all concerned if others chose to drink—that was up to them. It was just that he much preferred to get his highs naturally.

Taking his cold drink, he crossed over to the window and looked out at the lights of Westminster blinking below.

Why was he feeling so unsettled? Somehow he had become involved in another person's life, and that was something he'd sworn he'd never do. But he'd never felt so drawn to a woman before. She was beautiful, there was no doubt about that, but he had dated more beautiful woman than her and he'd never felt the need to make them part of his life. At least, not a permanent one.

When he was with Katie something deep inside him quietened and felt at peace.

Not that he was feeling peaceful right now. She made him think about stuff he didn't want to think about. Like his childhood. Making him feel that he was missing out somehow. That having someone in your life who cared might be a good thing. That he wanted to be a better man.

The thought scared him more than any cliff or big wave. He valued his independence too much. No, he was attracted to her because she was a lovely, kind woman who needed a friend. It was her vulnerability that was making him feel this way. That was all. He thought the realisation would make him feel better, but it didn't. Probably because he had the uneasy feeling he was lying to himself.

Later, after Fabio had dropped her off at home, Katie crept up to her room, thankful Suzy was in bed. She would only have to take one look at her face to know she'd been crying.

Katie thought about the evening. Fabio had been kind and understanding, and it had, she admitted, been a relief to finally talk to someone about Richard.

There was so much more to Fabio than she'd given him credit for. He was sensitive and thoughtful and easy to talk to. That connection that she'd felt almost as soon as they'd met was growing stronger every time they were together.

That wasn't all. When she was with him, she felt happy again. As if life had meaning once more. As if there was a future to believe in.

His presence banished the shadows from her life and her world came alight whenever he was around.

She groaned and buried her face in her hands. Despite everything she'd told herself, she was falling in love with him. She could no longer keep pretending to herself.

But that didn't change the type of man Fabio was or the reasons why she shouldn't let herself care more deeply about him than she already did. Not only was he a risk-taker, he'd made it very clear that he wasn't into serious relationships.

Remembering what Kendrick had said about big wave surfing, she logged onto her computer and ran a search. A link to a video clip came up and she clicked the play button. What she saw made her feel as if someone had dropped ice cubes down the back of her neck. A surfer was being towed by a jet ski out to the biggest wave Katie had ever seen. The surfer let go of the tow rope and proceeded to surf down a sea of water that looked the size of a mountain, or a six-storey building. Katie held her breath for the interminable seconds it took the surfer to ride the wave. Were they crazy? Anybody could see that all it would take was one wrong move and the surfer would be buried under a wave from which there was no hope of escape. According to the report, a crazy few extreme surfers went all over the world in search of exceptional waves that could only be reached by helicopter and jet ski. Ireland was one of those places.

As she watched the clip again, Katie's blood ran cold. Then she typed in 'BASE jumping', and if anything that made her feel worse. Only a week ago somebody had been killed during a jump. If ever she needed a reason to stay away from Fabio, this was it. No way could she ever trust her heart with someone who risked their life for fun. Why, then, did she feel as if someone had removed her heart and trampled all over it?

CHAPTER NINE

A COUPLE of days later, Fabio came to find Katie. She had gone out of her way to avoid him since the night of the premiere, terrified he'd read how she felt about him in her eyes.

He'd phoned to make sure she was all right, but they hadn't spoken since. At least, not about anything except work.

'I've just had Amelia on the phone. She's worried about Lucy. Says she's not her usual self. I'm going out to see her—are you free to come too?'

'Of course I'll come. I have one more patient then I'm all yours. I won't be more than thirty minutes. Will that be okay?'

Fabio nodded, looking worried. Despite his nonchalant manner, Katie had seen from the way he was with Lucy that the little girl was more to him than just a patient. She hoped Lucy hadn't caught a chest infection. Every time she did, it carried a risk of additional scarring to the lungs.

The more infections, the worse the ultimate prognosis. Not that there was anything anyone could do to stop a sufferer of CF getting chest infections. It was impossible unless the patient spent their life in a bubble and the effect on the quality of life had its own drawbacks.

Alone in the car with Fabio, Katie switched on the radio, pretending to find a news item fascinating. She needn't have worried. Fabio seemed preoccupied with his own thoughts.

Every time Katie went to Lucy's home she was stunned all over again. A little outside London, it had its own private gated entrance, enormous manicured gardens, a swimming pool and tennis courts.

Amelia met them at the door. If anything, she was paler than ever and for the first time Katie saw her looking less than immaculate. Her hair was scraped back in a ponytail and instead of her usual stylish trouser suits she was wearing a pair of jogging trousers and a T-shirt.

Fabio jumped out of his car as soon as it stopped and went over to Amelia.

'Hi, Amelia. Where's our patient?' he asked.

'Thank God you're both here. I didn't know

what to do. I wondered if I should take her straight to hospital, but when you said you could come, I knew it was better to wait.'

'Why don't I go and see her before we make any decisions?' Fabio asked. 'Is she in bed?'

Amelia nodded. 'That's how I know she isn't well. Normally I can't keep her inside, especially on a day like this.' She indicated the garden with a sweep of her hand. The June sunshine bathed everything in light, but Katie felt a shiver of dread.

Katie followed Amelia and Fabio up the sweeping staircase. She hoped that Amelia was being over-anxious, and who could blame her? But equally Amelia had enough experience of her daughter's illness to know when she should seek medical help.

Lucy was sitting up in bed, looking listlessly out of the window.

'Hey, Luce,' Fabio said, crossing the room. 'Mum tells me you're not feeling too good.'

'Hey, Dr Fabio,' Lucy replied softly. 'I'm just a bit tireder than usual. I told Mum I'll be all right by tomorrow.'

'I assume you've being having your physio

regularly? When Katie hasn't been doing it?' Since they'd returned from Monaco, Katie had been teaching Amelia and Lucy how to do Lucy's physio. Under Katie's supervision Amelia had soon gained the confidence to do it herself and they had agreed that they would do it themselves two days out of three, with Katie coming every third day.

Amelia nodded. 'If anything, Lucy has been having it more regularly since I can do it.'

'We all know that it is an unfortunate part of CF—that despite the medication and the physio chest infections can still occur,' Fabio said as he slipped a stethoscope from his bag. 'Why don't I listen to Lucy's chest and then we can see what's what?'

When Fabio finished his examination, he looked up and smiled. 'You do have a very mild chest infection, Luce, but I don't think it's too bad. I'm going to give you some antibiotics, up your dose of mucolytics and come back and see you tomorrow, but I think we caught it in time to get on top of it quite easily. In the meantime, I'm afraid, Lucy, you need to rest. Not necessarily in bed, though.'

'I could make you up a little bed on one of the couches outside by the swimming pool,' Amelia suggested. 'How about that?'

'I don't know, Mum. Maybe tomorrow.'

Fabio, Katie and Amelia looked at each other. This behaviour was unlike Lucy. Katie wondered if something else was bothering the little girl. Something she didn't want to share with her mother.

'Why don't I give you some physio while your mum and Dr Fabio have a chat?' Katie suggested. Perhaps if she got Lucy on her own she might share whatever it was that was troubling her.

'Okay, sweetie, do you want to tell me what's really up?' Katie asked as she percussed Lucy's chest.

Lucy was quiet for a moment. 'There's this girl at school. I thought she was my friend.' Katie waited for her to continue. 'She said she overheard her mum and dad talking about me.' Lucy's bottom lip wobbled and her eyes were damp. Katie stopped what she was doing and sat on the bed alongside Lucy and put her arm around her.

'Go on, Luce. You can tell me. What did she hear?'

'Her mum's a doctor. I don't know what kind. Anyway, they were saying that they were sorry for Mum. That not only might she lose me but even if I did live into my thirties she would probably never know what it was like to have grandchildren because I would almost certainly never be able to have babies.'

'Oh, sweetie,' Katie squeezed her tighter. 'We don't know that.'

'I don't even know how you have babies,' Lucy said, 'but I think one day I'll want to be a mummy.' She was quiet for another moment. 'I'm sorry for Mum and Dad too. I know that I make them sad. I don't want to make them even sadder if I can't have babies.'

For a moment Katie couldn't think of anything to say. What was there to say? Children with cystic fibrosis often did have trouble conceiving, but many went on to have perfectly healthy pregnancies. At this stage only time would tell. Lucy was far too young to have to worry about stuff like that at the moment, but on the other hand she was wiser than her years and didn't deserve to be palmed off. How could she give the child the comfort she needed right now? Only by telling her the truth.

'We don't know how your illness is going to progress, Luce. What I do know is that medical science is making huge advances in the treatment of CF every day. All we can do is try to keep you as healthy as we can and trust that you are going to lead a long life that includes all you ever dreamed of. I wish I could promise you right now that everything will be okay, but I can't. What I do know for sure is that your mum and dad love you very much and that they would rather have you the way you are than a different child. As for thinking that you make them sad, you don't. You bring so much joy and happiness to their lives you should be proud. Of course I know that if they could take away your illness with a magic wand, if they could do anything to make you better, they would. But if it is a choice between having you, Lucy, and not having you at all, there's no contest.'

Katie hugged Lucy tighter. 'You know, Luce, one day you'll meet someone and fall in love.' She smiled as Lucy pulled a face. 'And if he's worth loving he will want to share his life with you regardless of whether you can have children or not. That's the important thing to remember.'

Lucy smiled wanly. Then, in the way of children, she picked up her games console and eased her legs out of bed.

'I think I'll do as Mum suggested and rest outside by the pool.'

'You should tell your mum and dad what you told me,' Katie said, helping Lucy into her dressing gown. 'They will be able to reassure you.'

'Maybe.' She flung her arms around Katie and squeezed her so tightly Katie stumbled back a step or two.

'Whoa, Lucy. You're stronger than you think.' But Katie was delighted to see that Lucy's apathy seemed to have disappeared. For the time being at least. No doubt there would be many times over the coming years when the child would have to face up to the effects of her illness. However, she was a tough kid and somehow Katie knew she would deal with whatever life threw at her.

'C'mon, then.' Lucy smiled. 'Let's go and see if Mum has a snack for us.'

* * *

After they had driven away, leaving Lucy tucked up on the sofa outside with Amelia reading to her, Fabio turned to Katie.

'What happened back there? One minute Lucy was looking miserable, the next she was more like herself.'

'We had a chat while I was doing her physio,' Katie said. 'It seems that some kid at school said something about her not being able to have children.'

'*Porra!*' Fabio said. 'Poor kid. How did you deal with it?'

'The only way I knew how. I told her that it was far too early for anyone to know whether her illness would affect her fertility—not in those exact words, though. I said that when she grows up and meets someone who falls in love with her, if he's any kind of man at all, he won't care whether she can have children.'

Katie slid a glance in Fabio's direction. He was frowning as he concentrated on the road ahead.

'A small percentage of children do suffer fertility problems,' he said after a while. 'It is something Lucy might well have to face later on.'

'It's so unfair. The way life can turn out for some people,' Katie muttered.

'One thing I do know, Katie, is we have to make the best of what we have. Life can be fun and exciting and we should make the most of any time we might have.'

'Is that why you go big wave surfing and BASE jumping, or whatever they call it. Just for the excitement? Don't you care that you could be killed?' Katie burst out.

Fabio held her gaze for a second. 'Of course for the excitement. What other reason could there be? I am not planning on getting myself killed, though. I manage the risk.'

'Manage the risk! From what I saw on the internet, there is no way you can manage the risk. Too many things can go wrong. Men like you just don't think.' She couldn't help it. She was so frightened for him. Not that she could admit it.

Fabio brought his car to a stop and swivelled in his seat.

'You looked it up on the internet?' His lips twitched briefly.

Damn. She hadn't meant to say that, but he was always doing strange things to her head.

'You're really upset, aren't you?' he continued with wonder in his voice. Then a look of remorse crossed his face. 'Of course you're thinking about your brother. But, Katie, this is different. I really don't take crazy chances.'

Anger was still boiling up inside her. Not least because she was furious with herself for showing him that she cared. 'What you do has nothing to do with me. If you want to break your damned neck, that's entirely up to you.'

Despite her best efforts, hot tears were burning behind her eyes. She looked out of her side window and blinked rapidly. *Please. Don't let me make a bigger fool of myself than I've done already.*

'Katie,' he said softly. 'I warned you not to care about me. I'm not the kind of man you need.'

When she said nothing—he wasn't to know she couldn't speak—he started the car and headed back into the traffic.

After Fabio dropped Katie off at home he sat in his car for a while, drumming his fingers on the steering-wheel, feeling restless.

He wondered what Katie would think if he told

her that he had suffered from the effects of having mumps as a child. Not that he intended to tell her. It wasn't as if he had any plans to get married and have children. But she would one day and that was the problem. Whatever she'd told Lucy about not caring whether someone could have kids when you were in love with them was naïve. Surely that was the only reason most people got married? Otherwise why bother?

He glanced at his watch. Six o'clock. It would be daylight for another hour or so. Not for the first time he wished he lived closer to the sea. Taking a board out and pitching himself against the waves, or flinging himself off a cliff, always helped clear his head, but that would have to wait to the weekend. Perhaps he would go for a ten-mile run. Maybe after that he would be able to sleep without thinking of sad grey eyes and a wounded expression.

Fabio, with Kendrick behind him on his surf-board, drove the jet ski at speed towards the wave. It was one of a set of five and Kendrick was determined to ride the wave of his life. After he had finished it would be Fabio's turn. The wind rushed through him, filling him with exhilaration. This was just what he needed to get Katie out of his head. The ten-mile run the night before hadn't helped him to get to sleep or prevent his dreams from being filled with Katie.

Kendrick had hired a helicopter to take them to the west coast of Ireland, where he'd heard that the waves were, in his words, 'awesome'. He'd been right. There was no way they could catch the waves by paddling out to them—hence the need for the jet ski.

Fabio towed Kendrick on to the lip of the second wave and raced the jet ski out of the way. As he turned back to watch, he felt a sickening jolt of dread. Kendrick was in trouble. The drop of the wave was so huge there would be no time for his cousin to surf under the curling lip of the wave before it crashed down on him.

It seemed that this time they had taken one risk too many.

His heart pounding, Fabio watched as Kendrick did the only thing he could—he dived straight into the wave, hoping to come out the other side. But it wasn't to be. The wave hit Kendrick with such force it sent him and his board shooting into the air.

Fabio gunned the jet ski and headed back towards his cousin. Kendrick had been hit by his board and was bobbing around semi-conscious. Summoning all his strength, Fabio grabbed the neck of Kendrick's wetsuit and dragged him onto the front of the jet ski. He had to get him to dry land before he could assess how badly his cousin was hurt. He glanced around for help but knew it was useless. There was no one else crazy enough to tackle the waves that morning.

It seemed to take for ever to drag Kendrick back to shore. Once he was as close to the beach as he could manage, he still had to get him onto to the beach and Kendrick was a big man.

To his relief, Kendrick was coming round.

Fabio cut the engine of his jet ski, hoping that the tide wouldn't pull them back out.

'Kendrick!' he yelled in his cousin's ear. 'Are you with me?'

Kendrick groaned and opened his eyes. 'Hey, man, what happened?'

'Can you wade to shore?'

Kendrick pushed himself off the jet ski and

although he swayed a little he managed to stay upright long enough for Fabio to jump into the water and get his arm around him for support. Together they staggered to shore and collapsed on the beach.

Fabio took a look at Kendrick's head. It was bleeding but should only require a stitch or two. Fabio knew it was only a matter of luck that they were both still in one piece.

Kendrick eased himself to his feet and smiled down at Fabio.

'Some wave. D'you fancy giving it a go?'

For the first time Fabio wondered what he was doing. He would always love the excitement of pitching himself against nature but, hell, he didn't want to die.

'You, my friend, are going nowhere—except to the hospital, where we can get that head wound stitched,' Fabio said.

Kendrick looked as if he was about to argue, but then he grinned. 'Okay, but once I'm fixed up, can we go back in?'

As Fabio waited in Casualty a little while later for Kendrick to be fixed up, he knew that he would be going back to London that evening.

For some reason, big wave surfing had lost its appeal. Perhaps it was because Katie wasn't there. Perhaps it was because these days he was getting more of a buzz by being with her than any extreme sport could give him. The realisation turned his blood to ice. Damn the woman, he couldn't stop thinking about her, wanting to be with her. What was going on? Lust had never done this to him before. *Deus!* He was falling for Katie Simpson and he didn't like the feeling one little bit. All he knew for sure was that he had to see her.

CHAPTER TEN

KATIE was taken aback when on Saturday evening she opened the door to find Fabio standing there.

'Will you have dinner with me tonight?' he said.

Katie's heart did a little roll of beats. When he smiled like that, it undid her.

'I'm sorry, I can't. I promised Suzy I'd babysit. She's going out with a friend for the first time since…' Her words tailed away.

He looked disappointed and uncharacteristically unsure of himself.

'But there's no reason why I can't cook for us here,' Katie said impulsively. 'If you like baby food, that is. I don't think there's very much else.'

'Tell you what. Why don't I cook?'

When he grinned at her, Katie knew astonishment was written all over her face. Fabio could cook?

'I know it's a surprise, but I can make a mean feijoada. It's a typical Brazilian dish.'

'What's in it?'

He grinned again and if anything Katie's heart beat faster.

'You'll find out,' he said. 'Give me an hour and I'll be back.'

After he'd left Katie leaned against the door. He was making it clear that he was interested in her and the realisation churned her up inside.

'Was that Fabio's voice I heard?' Suzy came into the room, towelling her hair. Although her sister-in-law's eyes were still shadowed with grief, she was beginning to go out with her friends again, and was even talking about returning to work. And as for her? She still couldn't think of Richard without experiencing a stab of pain that took her breath away, but since the night she'd confided in Fabio, she was beginning to see a future that wasn't clouded by grief.

'I've invited him here for dinner,' Katie said. When Suzy's eyebrows shot up, Katie added hastily. 'He's doing the cooking.'

'Just as well. Although you have many talents, my dear sister-in-law, cooking isn't one of them.'

'I can make pasta. And toasted sandwiches,'

Katie protested, before answering the smile in Suzy's eyes. 'Okay, so he's had a narrow escape.'

'He likes you,' Suzy said.

Katie's heart kicked against her ribs.

'You don't know that.'

'I think I do. What's there not to like? You're beautiful and kind—okay, you can't cook but, hey, we can't all be perfect.'

Katie turned away. 'He's just being a caring colleague, that's all. Anyway, he's not for me.'

Suzy studied her thoughtfully as if she knew Katie was lying. 'He's gorgeous, rich, a great doctor, and he cooks. What's not to like?'

Katie sighed. There was no point pretending with Suzy. She'd always been able to read her like a book.

'He does make me laugh. More than that, he turns me to jelly. But he's reckless and a womaniser. He's made it crystal clear he's not interested in a serious relationship. I don't want to fall in love with someone like him. One way or another, he'll end up breaking my heart.' The words came out almost like a wail. 'I'm sorry, I don't know where that came from. I'm just so emotional these days. I've had enough grief in my life without inviting more.' Katie picked up some toys and baby odds and ends from the floor and dropped them into a basket.

'Something tells me it might be too late,' Suzy said, so softly Katie couldn't be sure she'd heard right. 'Why not just go with the flow? Have a fling. Have fun. God knows, you could do with some of that in your life right now.'

'But I work with him, Suze. It's not a good idea to have a fling—as you so quaintly put it—with a work colleague. And you know me. I'm not the fling type.'

Suzy smiled. 'Maybe it's about time you were.'

After Suzy had left, Katie finished tidying up before showering, taking the time to shave her legs and wash her hair. Whatever Suzy said, she was so not going to have a fling with Fabio. This was dinner with a colleague. What could possibly happen when there was a child in the house? Katie had to smile at the thought of using her nephew to keep Fabio at arm's length. What kind of wimp did that make her? But she'd do whatever it took. Ricky was sleeping through the night now and was unlikely to wake up, but just in case she was careful to keep the baby monitor switched on and close by.

Now, what should she wear? Something that didn't scream date but that she felt good in. Eventually she settled on the sundress she had worn that night on the yacht.

She had only finished putting the finishing touches to her make-up when Fabio arrived back, carrying bags of shopping. Judging from the faint scent of spice and lemon, somehow he too had found time to shower and change. He was wearing tight, faded jeans and an open-necked white silk shirt. Katie's throat went dry at the sight of him.

'Just put the bags over on the worktop,' she said, leading him through to the kitchen. 'Would you like something to drink?'

Fabio shook his head. 'I don't drink and anyway I'm driving, but feel free to have one yourself.'

Katie poured herself a glass of cold white Pinot Grigio from the fridge and took a bigger gulp than she'd intended, spluttering as it went down the wrong way.

'Are you all right?' Fabio asked, patting her on the back.

She nodded. Great start. Here she was with the most sophisticated man she had ever met and she couldn't even manage to take a sip of her drink without choking.

'Okay,' he said, pointing to a bar stool by the counter. 'You sit there, well out of danger's way, while I get cooking.'

'Don't you want a hand?' she asked.

His mouth tipped in a smile. 'I can cope. I hope you like Brazilian food.'

'Can't say I've ever tried it, but I'd like to.' She squinted at him. 'Tell me more about Brazil. What's it like? Do you go there much?'

'Not as much as I should, but I'm thinking of taking a trip there in a week or two to see my mother.'

Katie felt a thud of dismay. She hated the thought of not being able to see him most days.

'And as for as what it's like, you should visit one day.'

A glow spread through Katie. Did he mean that? Impossible though it seemed, was he envisaging a future for them? She dismissed the thought. Hadn't she told herself repeatedly Fabio was not for her? Why couldn't her heart keep in tune with her head?

'We have the greatest footballers in the world,' he continued as he assembled the ingredients he'd brought.

Katie hid her disappointment. Was she always going to be reading more into his words than he intended?

She rolled her eyes. 'Don't tell me you're one of those men who can't bear to miss a match.'

'You are kidding! Unless I can't help it, I never miss a game.'

'There must be more to Brazil than football.'

'A lot more. You'd love it. Think of the clearest seas, white sands, palm trees, and you've pretty much got it.' He paused his stirring and looked at her. 'Not that it's paradise. As I told you before, there's a huge difference between the rich and poor that is almost scandalous.'

'How did your parents feel about you becoming a doctor?'

'They were a little surprised, I think, but doctors are held in high esteem in Brazil so they didn't think it was too much of a drop in status,' he said with a twist to his lips. 'Besides I suspect they thought I'd give it up sooner or later.'

'Tell me more about your mother. I know she's stunningly beautiful, but what's she really like?'

Fabio placed the lid on the pot and leaned back against the counter, studying her through narrowed eyes.

'My mother? Yes, she is beautiful. Even in her late fifties. But I guess I don't really know her that well. She wasn't around that much when I was a child. When she and Dad split up, they divided my time between them, but that didn't work in too well with their careers so they found me a boarding school.'

'That must have been difficult.'

Fabio's expression darkened. 'Not half as difficult as it was living with them both, witnessing them tear each other apart.' Although he smiled, it didn't quite reach his eyes. 'Enough of that. What do you mean, you don't understand the rules of football?'

Katie was just clearing away the dishes from the dining table when she heard Ricky cry. 'If you want to go to him, I'll finish here,' Fabio said.

Katie picked Ricky up and quickly changed his wet nappy. He was due a feed and Suzy had left a bottle in the fridge to be warmed up. Carrying the crying baby over her shoulder, she went into the kitchen, where Fabio was stacking dishes on the counter. Amused, she noticed he wasn't quite domesticated enough to put them directly into the dishwasher, but that was okay. His cooking had been a treat.

'You couldn't hold him while I warm his bottle, could you?' she asked.

'Sure,' Fabio said, taking Ricky from her. 'How are you, little man?' As she set about warming the bottle she looked over at Fabio and her heart lurched. His dark head was bent over Ricky, who had grabbed Fabio's ear and was tugging it as if he wanted it to come off. Her heart splintered. There was something about this man, who radiated masculinity on the one hand yet wasn't scared to show a gentler side, that she couldn't resist.

Having warmed the bottle, Katie took Ricky back from Fabio and made herself comfortable in one of the armchairs. As the baby sucked greedily on his bottle, she looked up to find Fabio's eyes on her. He was watching her with a strange, inscrutable expression.

'What?' she asked.

He shook his head. 'Nothing.' He turned away and looked out of the window. 'I think it's time I was going,' he said.

Katie was disappointed, but who could blame him? Fabio wasn't someone who would be comfortable in a scenario of domestic bliss. He was more at home in a posh bar. When she saw him glance at his watch she wondered if he was planning to drop in at some club before going home. That was much more his scene.

'Thank you for dinner,' she said. 'I had a lovely time.'

'I'll let myself out, shall I?' he said, and before Katie could respond she heard the soft click of the door as it closed behind him.

Fabio paced his flat. This was becoming a habit, he thought grimly. The more time he spent with Katie, the less the idea of late nights and bars appealed to him.

The image of her sitting in the armchair with

Ricky in her arms just wouldn't go away. It had looked so right, so natural.

Then again, everything about her was so natural. Whenever he was with her he felt as if he were in an oasis of peace and calm, and when he wasn't, he felt like this; restless and out of sorts.

In another life, he would have wooed her, but what did he have to offer? No doubt one day she'd want children of her own and it wasn't as if he could give her a family. And as for being dependent on someone else to make him happy—well, since he'd been a child and had had to get used to dealing with life on his own, he'd promised he would never rely on anyone and, more importantly, not let anyone depend on him. He was happy the way he was. Wasn't he?

He drained his orange juice in a gulp. For a second he thought about phoning Fern but only for a second. These days other women had lost their appeal. His mind kept returning to Katie and the sight of her with the baby. He had never given children much thought, knowing it was almost certainly impossible. But, for the first time, he wondered whether there was a chance. Things had moved on since he was eighteen. The way his mind was going jolted him. Thinking of babies and families. All because of one grey-eyed woman. Had he lost his mind?

CHAPTER ELEVEN

As the days continued to pass, Suzy and Katie settled into a routine. Suzy and little Ricky were her family now and Kate felt closer to Richard just by being with his wife and child.

Fabio remained friendly but distant and every time Katie caught a glimpse of his dark head her stomach would flip. He hadn't asked her out again and she wasn't sure if she was disappointed or relieved. However, it was better this way.

One day as she was tidying up her treatment room he sought her out.

'Mark and Amelia are hoping to take Lucy with them for Turkish Grand Prix in Istanbul and were wondering whether you and I would go with them.'

Katie kept her back towards him. More time with Fabio wasn't really what she needed. On the other hand, this was why she'd been employed by the practice.

'When?' she asked. 'I'll have to check my patient list.'

'This weekend. I know it's unfair to ask you to give up your free time, but Amelia and Mark would appreciate it.' Fabio said. 'You could take time off at the beginning of the week to make up for it. Jenny would be happy to shuffle your diary around.'

Katie hesitated and then gave herself a little shake. She couldn't let personal feelings get in the way of her doing her job.

'I don't mind about working over the weekend and I was a little worried about Lucy's chest the last time I saw her. Do you think it's wise to let her go?'

'You know how Lucy feels about being able to do things with her parents. I'll be there to keep a close eye on her and you'll be there to do her physio. In many ways she couldn't get better care, even if she was in hospital. Amelia and Mark would be really grateful if you could go. Amelia only decided to go yesterday. Apparently, if Mark wins this one, and there's a good chance he will, then he's in the lead. They really want to see him do that.'

Boy, did Fabio know which buttons to press. He knew she couldn't refuse Lucy the opportunity to see her father. 'In which case, I can't say no, can I?' She was mortified to hear a touch of bitterness in her voice.

He placed a hand on her elbow and turned her so she was facing him. 'What is it, Katie? Something's up. Is it Suzy?'

How could she tell him that she didn't want to spend more time with him than necessary? How could she tell him that seeing him every day was torture?

Of course she couldn't.

She forced a smile. 'Nothing's wrong, honestly.' She should cross her fingers behind her back. 'Istanbul it is.'

And so, once again, Katie found herself ensconced in Mark's private jet. As before, they would be staying on board the yacht that Mark's sponsors had put at his disposal. Despite her reservations, Katie was excited. And, she had to admit, happy knowing that she would be with Fabio for a few days.

'Have you ever been to Istanbul?' he asked as they took off.

'To be honest, I've never been very far. I travelled around Europe with friends from university, but that's it really. What about you?' She smiled at him. 'I guess you've been everywhere.'

'Most places, but not Turkey. It's always somewhere I wanted to go, though.' He studied her from under his long, dark lashes. 'Maybe you and I could see some of the sights together?'

Katie's heart thrummed. She wanted to be with him, even though it was bitter-sweet. She hauled out her guide book and flicked it open. 'As a matter of fact, I've earmarked a couple of places I would like to see. The Haghia Sophia, of course, the Basilica Cistern, the Blue Mosque and the Topkapi Palace—and that's just for starters. I've been reading up about the Ottoman Empire since I knew I'd be making this trip and I'd like to see as much as I can squeeze in. I guess it depends whether Lucy wants to go too, or if she'd prefer to hang out with her parents.'

They chatted about what Katie had learned in the guidebook for a while, then she yawned.

'I think I'll nap for a bit, if you don't mind.

Ricky was a bit unsettled last night. He's teething, we think, poor lamb.'

She rested her head and closed her eyes, wondering if she would be able to sleep. Despite her tiredness, every nerve in her body was intensely aware of Fabio next to her. She wanted to ask him to go and sit on the other side of the plane, but that would be ridiculous. She could hardly explain that his close proximity unnerved her to the point of not being able to think. Her thoughts drifted. She and Fabio were somewhere alone, a picnic perhaps, he was looking at her as if he loved her…

As Katie's breathing slowed to a regular rhythm Fabio studied her. Her long blonde hair had fallen over her face and she had a small smile on her face as if she was having happy dreams. She made his heart ache.

He loved the way everything excited her. She couldn't feign boredom if she tried. He still found it difficult to sleep at night. Every time he closed his eyes, her image would appear. Either laughing at some idiotic joke he'd made in an attempt to keep the sparkle in her eyes, or her face awash with sadness as if she was remembering her brother.

He was tempted to brush back the stray lock of hair that had fallen across her eyes, and only just managed to restrain himself. However he felt about this woman, it wouldn't be fair to start anything. Katie wasn't the kind of woman to fall in love easily and somehow he knew with un-shakable certainty that when she did, it would be for ever. She would want children one day and if the thought that it wouldn't be with him made his stomach clench, that was too bad. He was many things, but selfish wasn't one of them.

The yacht was moored in the Bosphorus. By the time they stepped on board it was dark and the river twinkled with a thousand lights.

The sights, sounds and smells of Istanbul hit her the moment they arrived. It was as if she had been transported to the Ottoman period when the sultans had lived in palaces.

'I can just imagine the sultans and their wives living here,' Katie breathed, as Amelia pointed out the Blue Mosque.

'You should visit the harem in Topkapi Palace

if you want to see what it was like for the women at that time. I'm not so sure it was all that great for them,' Amelia said, before kissing her. 'Thank you both again for coming. I know you didn't have to, but it means so much to Mark that Lucy and I can be here.'

Amelia looked more relaxed than the last time Katie had seen her. Lucy had been keeping well and she knew Amelia put that down to the care the little girl received.

'I intend to see as much as I can squeeze in. Maybe tomorrow? Do you think Lucy would like to come too?'

Lucy was in bed when they arrived, having travelled with her mother the day before.

Amelia laughed. 'I'm not sure going around museums is my daughter's cup of tea. But you can ask her yourself tomorrow. Maybe we'll all go while Mark is practising.'

In the end, as her mother suspected, Lucy had decided not to come. ''S boring,' she said. 'But you can go, Mum. I'll be all right by myself.'

'Of course I'm not going to go without you. Anyway, I've seen it before.'

'Then I'll stay too,' Katie offered. She'd already

carried out some physio on Lucy and had been pleased to see that her home routine was working well. Lucy's chest was clear. At least for the time being.

'No. You and Fabio go off for the day. At least if you're both seeing something of Istanbul, I won't feel too bad about dragging you out here on your weekend off.'

'I'd hardly call it dragging,' Katie protested.

'Still, I insist you go. Enjoy your day and we'll see you back here for drinks before dinner.'

The tender that belonged to the yacht dropped Katie and Fabio off at the harbour. It was thronged with tourists thumbing through travel guides and locals selling every imaginable delicacy from small stalls. In every way it was different from the sophisticated glitz of Monte Carlo, but Katie decided she liked it better. It was more authentic.

'Okay, where do you want to go first?' Fabio asked.

'I don't know—anywhere. Everywhere.'

'Okay, put yourself in my hands,' Fabio said, taking her by the hand. Katie felt herself go crimson. Whether it was because of the image that popped into her head of her in Fabio's hands, or whether it was because the feeling of her fingers in his was so deliciously secure, she wasn't sure.

Fabio steered her across the road. The cars made no attempt to slow down for them and Katie was relieved when, after dodging the traffic, they made it to the other side in one piece.

They went first to the famous Blue Mosque that dominated the city. Katie read snippets from the guide book as they roamed the impressive building with its thousands of blue tiles that gave it its name. After that they visited the underground Basilica to gawp at the hundreds of pillars and Medusa's head before heading to the Topkapi Palace. Fabio stopped outside to buy her some cut-up watermelon to quench their thirst and they sat on a bench, taking in the sights and sounds.

'It says here that the sultan kept as many as three hundred concubines in his harem,' Katie said. 'A bit much for most men, don't you think?'

Fabio grinned at her, his eyes creasing at the corners.

'I guess it depends on the women,' he teased.

'I suspect you would have been in your element,' Katie said grumpily. 'A different woman for almost every day of the year.'

'That's a bit unfair,' Fabio said. Before she knew it he had taken a lock of her hair and tucked it behind her ear. 'I think if the sultan or whoever met the right woman, she would be enough for him. I know it would be for me.'

Her heart was hammering so hard in her chest Katie thought it might explode. If she hadn't known better she would have sworn that his eyes were full of meaning…and longing. But that was silly. If Fabio felt anything for her, he would have said—or done—something.

'Shall we go in?' she suggested, relieved to hear her voice was steady. As she got to her feet she found her legs were less so.

Fabio stood and kissed her lightly on the lips. '*Vamos!* Let's go!'

As he turned away Katie put a finger on her lips where his had been only moments before.

Damn, damn, damn. Why did she have to be falling for this man? Her heart stopped. *Falling* in love? She could no longer fool herself. Her heart had been no match for her head. She'd fallen hook, line and sinker. For ever.

After they had admired everything the palace had to offer, they stopped at the harbour for a fish sandwich. As Fabio watched Katie happily perched on a makeshift stool, eagerly waiting for her fish, caught only moments before, to be grilled and placed between two slices of bread, his heart cracked. She was everything he'd ever wanted in a woman, but hadn't known he did until he'd met her. Why did she have to come into his life when he'd thought he was happy? And now he knew he hadn't been. The restless-ness, the constant seeking for new adventure, new thrills, new women had been a desperate attempt to fill the emptiness inside him that, until he'd met Katie, he hadn't realised was there. He wanted her more than he'd ever wanted a woman before. Not just in his bed, but in his life. But he couldn't have her. It wasn't fair to Katie.

Back on the yacht, Lucy was waiting excitedly, keen to hear about their day and to tell them about hers.

'I went on the small boat all the way up the river. It was so much fun. Mum came too. And then one of the crew brought his son to meet me. He didn't speak much English, but he knew how to play computer games.'

Fabio ruffled her hair. 'Sounds like you had a good day, sweetie. How are you feeling?'

Katie glanced at Fabio.

'I'm feeling good,' Lucy said.

'Then you won't mind if I listen to your chest later just to make sure,' Fabio said. Katie had also noticed that Lucy's breathing was more laboured than usual. Perhaps the humidity was affecting her chest. She desperately hoped it wasn't the first signs of a chest infection.

'I'm okay,' Lucy said, setting her mouth in a firm line.

'Mark and I have been invited to dinner with the rest of the team tonight,' Amelia said. 'You and Fabio are invited too.'

Katie rubbed her feet. They were aching from all the walking they had done that day. 'If you don't mind, I think I'll give it a miss. I'm shattered.'

'What about you ,Fabio?'

'Me? Oh, if it's okay with you, I think I'll stay here too. Keep Katie and Lucy company.'

'But I want to go to dinner with you and Daddy,' Lucy protested. 'Please, Mum. Can I?'

Amelia smiled at her daughter. 'If Fabio thinks it's okay and you're not too tired, of course you can come. But...' she wagged a finger at her daughter's smiling face '...you'll have to leave early. I want you in bed by ten at the latest.'

Lucy pouted but it was only for a moment. ''Kay,' she said. 'I'll probably get bored unless there's a kid my age to play with.'

Amelia puckered her brow. 'Would it be okay if I gave the staff the evening off? I usually do when we're all off the yacht, but I could ask the chef to stay behind and make you dinner before he joins the others.'

Fabio and Katie shook their heads in unison.

'Not really hungry...' Katie said.

'I can make supper,' Fabio said at the same time. Their eyes locked and Katie felt the air fizz between them. She wanted to be alone with him and it seemed he felt the same way.

'No.' Katie smiled. 'Don't worry about us. Have a good time.'

Fabio stood and stretched. '*Vamos*, Lucy. Let's check you over before Katie gives you your physio. We want you to be in tip-top condition for your evening out.'

When Fabio and Lucy left to go below, Amelia sighed.

'He's so good with her. I don't know how we would have coped without him these last couple of years.'

'You would have managed fine.'

Amelia shook her head. 'Until Fabio became her doctor, I wouldn't let Lucy do anything. I was always so scared. Mark was always asking us both to come and watch him race, but I was too nervous that Lucy would get sick while we were abroad.' She smiled wanly. 'Silly, isn't it? Most countries where Mark races have perfectly good hospitals, but it's not the same somehow.'

'No, I guess it isn't. Not that I'd know. I haven't travelled much before. Apart from a trip to Europe with friends from university and going to Monaco and coming here, I've always holidayed at home.'

Amelia took a sip of her drink. 'Are you seeing someone? Is that why you don't travel?'

Katie shook her head. 'I've never met anyone I've wanted to be with.' Until now, a small voice whispered inside her head. 'At least, not longer than six months.'

'What about Fabio?' Amelia asked with a teasing smile. 'You two seem pretty close.'

'Fabio!' Katie tried to fix an expression on her face as if it was the first time such a thought had crossed her mind. Unfortunately she could feel a tell-tale blush creep up her cheeks. 'Fabio and I are just colleagues.'

Amelia's smile told Katie that she wasn't fooled, but without saying anything else Amelia drained the last of her drink and got to her feet. 'I should go and shower and change, if I'm not going to be late.' She frowned at her watch. 'I wonder where Mark is? He should be back by now.' She sighed. 'I guess he must be chatting to his team.'

Although Amelia's words were light, Katie could see the anxiety lurking behind her eyes. Once again she thought of how much she'd hate to be in Amelia's shoes. It must be hell on earth wondering whether your husband was going to come back to you in one piece, however much Amelia claimed to be used to it.

'Would you mind telling Luce that I'll come and help her get ready in a bit?' Amelia said.

'I'll go and tell her now. Fabio will have finished checking her over, I'm sure.'

Katie found Lucy and Fabio sitting on Lucy's bed, arguing over a game on Lucy's games console. Katie suppressed a smile. Sometimes she wondered who was the biggest kid. Despite what Fabio had told her about not wanting children, he was a natural with them. Someday he would change his mind. At the thought her heart contracted. Fabio with a wife and children wasn't something she wanted to think about.

'Sorry to break this up, guys. But if you're going to have time to get ready for dinner, Luce, we should get on with your physio.'

Reluctantly Lucy put her game to the side. 'I was beating Fabio.'

'Were not. At least, I would have caught up eventually.'

'How is Lucy's chest?' Katie asked.

'A tiny bit more rattly than we would like, but nothing major. I've increased her antibiotics slightly and the physio should help.' He chucked

Lucy under the chin. 'I'll leave you two girls to it. Remember to come and show me yourself in all your finery.'

He glanced at Katie. 'I thought we could eat about eight? I'll go and see what the chef has in the fridge.'

Later after everyone had left—Mark had been late but thankfully intact—Katie was unsure what to do with the couple of hours before dinner.

There was no sign of Fabio, who had disappeared once Lucy had modelled her dress for him, and Katie eyed the hot tub longingly. The light was fading, although it was still warm. A few minutes in the tub would be good before she got ready for the evening.

This time she'd remembered to bring her costume and, nipping down to her cabin, she changed quickly, and went back up on deck, taking the white robe that had been left behind the door for her with her.

As she slipped into the hot water she sighed with pleasure. It was just the right temperature. She switched on the bubbles and rested her head against the tub rim and closed her eyes. Bliss.

'Do you mind if I join you?' At the sound of Fabio's voice, her eyes snapped open. He was standing in front of her, wearing his swimming shorts and holding a towel.

For a moment their eyes locked and Katie couldn't look away. She should get out, run for her life but her limbs felt heavy, weighted down. Her eyes were drawn to his chest, the way his swimming shorts hugged his hips, the dark silky hair on his lower abdomen. Hot sparks of desire were shot through her body. Knowing that if she tried to speak her voice would betray her, she simply nodded.

She closed her eyes again as he got into the tub. Although the tub could comfortably have held ten and there was plenty of space for him on the other side, he lowered his body onto the seat next to her.

She opened one eye and glanced at him. He was looking at her as if trying to memorise her face. Darkness fell and the moonlight seemed to light his eyes from within. The air between them fizzed and, as her heart leaped to her throat, Katie knew that she had been waiting for this moment all her life. A heady sense of inevitability drove any thoughts of danger from her head.

'Minha linda...' His voice was hoarse. 'What are you doing to me? Why can't I get you out of my head?'

She didn't want to be out of his head. She wanted stay there for the rest of her life. She wanted to be with him for ever. It was no use. She loved him. Hopelessly and for ever. Right or wrong—it no longer mattered.

He raised his hand and very gently pushed a lock of wet hair from her eyes. 'You know I want you, don't you? More than I thought it was possible to want a woman.'

Her heart was pounding so hard she thought he must be able to hear it.

He ran his hands down her face, letting them rest on either side of her neck. Slowly, ever so slowly, he brought his lips down on hers.

His mouth was warm and his lips soft—at first. He nibbled at her bottom lip then his kiss deepened and he explored her mouth with his tongue as if he couldn't get enough of her.

She kissed him back hungrily, tasting coffee and mint. Her head was spinning, her body straining towards him. He lifted his head and looked into her eyes.

'You are very beautiful,' he said huskily. 'Like a sea sprite.' His accent had thickened, his Brazilian accent coming to the fore.

He slid an arm underneath her bottom and lifted her onto his lap. She could feel his desire for her through the thin material of his swimming shorts.

It didn't matter that there was no future for them. All that mattered was the here and now and her aching need for him.

He pushed the top of her bikini away with his mouth and nuzzled her breasts. She threw her head back as a wall of desire took her breath away. She had never felt like this before. As if she was going to explode. As if she had no control over her body or her mind. She pulled back, terrified of the way her body reacted to him.

'It's okay, my love. It will be all right. I promise. Just give in to it.'

Trusting him, she gave herself up to the sensations. She could do nothing else.

He circled her nipple with his tongue and she moaned.

Then she gasped as his hand slid under her bikini. Involuntarily she parted her legs to give him better access.

He looked at her and as their eyes held, she was lost. She was drowning.

'Are you sure?' he asked.

She could only nod. She'd never been more sure of anything in her life.

'I think we should go somewhere less public,' he said hoarsely.

Taking her by the hand, he helped her out of the tub and down to his cabin. She could hardly breathe. Sensations were zinging around her body.

He'd barely kicked the door closed behind him before his hands were on her again. Touching, seeking out her secret places as he watched her response through half-closed lids. If he didn't finish what he'd started, she would scream with frustration.

He lifted her into his arms and laid her gently on the bed. His eyes glowed as he looked down at her. Reaching into a drawer, he pulled out a condom and lay down next to her.

Holding her gaze, he slipped his fingers inside

her. She cried out as wave upon wave of pleasure rocked her body.

Then with one swift movement he tugged off her bikini briefs and slipped out of his own.

He pulled her on top of him so that she was straddling him. He lifted her by the hips and then he was inside her and they were rocking together. She pushed back against his chest, wanting him, needing him deeper.

Once more he brought her to the edge where she cried out with her need, and then as he moaned and his thrusting became deeper, her body exploded with intense pleasure from the tips of her toes, coursing through her body right up to her scalp.

Gasping, they held each other. Katie felt her body turn to mush as the most incredible languid feeling spread through her body. She rested her head on his shoulder, hearing almost feeling his heart beating.

He stroked her hair wordlessly as she cuddled into him.

Suddenly shy, she buried her face in his shoulder. They stayed like that for a few more minutes,

Katie savouring the feeling of happiness as she listened to the rhythm of his heart.

He lifted her chin with his finger and looked deep into her eyes. His expression held a look of wonder. 'My God, Katie. What are you doing to me? I don't think I've ever wanted a woman as much as I want you.'

Want, not love. She pushed the words to the back of her mind. He hadn't made any promises. What was the point in worrying about the future when you couldn't control it anyway? She knew now that happiness had to be found wherever and whenever.

'I don't know about you,' Fabio said, 'but suddenly I'm starving.'

'Me too,' Katie whispered. 'I didn't realise sex could give you such an appetite.'

Fabio grinned down at her. 'We need to keep your strength up. I'm not finished with you yet.'

Her body tingled when he said the words. She wanted him again. She would never stop wanting him. This man was the person she'd been waiting for all her life. The other half of her soul. And if the thought made her ache with the knowledge he didn't share her feelings, hadn't she always known that she would only ever have a small part of him?

He eased himself off the bed and, despite what they had just shared, Katie blushed. He was so confident in his nakedness and why wouldn't he be? Every muscle was clearly defined without being too built up. His stomach was hard and flat, his legs long and lean.

Grinning at her scrutiny, he passed her his robe before wrapping a towel around his hips.

Still blushing furiously, Katie took the robe from him and slipped her arms in. Fabio took hold of the lapels of the robe and pulled her towards him. 'You have no idea how cute you look when you blush.' She shivered as he dropped a kiss on the side of her neck. If he carried on touching her, she would drag him back to bed.

Before she could act on the impulse, he released her and, taking her by the hand, led her back upstairs.

'The galley is in here. What do you fancy? Lobster? Langoustine? Something Turkish?' He opened the fridge with a flourish.

'Scrambled eggs will do me fine,' Katie said.

'That all?' he teased. 'I could eat a horse.'

Katie perched at the stainless-steel counter and watched Fabio as he whipped up some eggs and cut fresh bread. He looked perfectly at home. Was there anything this man couldn't do? Her body was still throbbing from the feel of him and she knew she wanted him again. She was in love with him, but he hadn't suggested she was anything except a casual fling. He had said lots of lovely things to her, but not that he cared about her. After this evening would he seek her out again, or would he be on to pastures new? Wasn't that how men like Fabio worked? Moving from one conquest to another? But she couldn't believe he didn't feel something for her. She'd seen the look in his eyes when he'd thought she wasn't watching and she'd seen the naked pain. That didn't fit with a man who didn't care.

If he had made no promises, neither had she. She should give it time. Wait and see.

Fabio piled creamy eggs onto a plate and passed it to her before doing the same to another plate and sitting down opposite her.

'I thought you'd be having something more substantial,' she said.

'And I found I lost my appetite. Funnily

enough, I have other things on my mind.' He leaned across and removed a morsel of egg that had landed on the side of her mouth and popped it into her mouth before running his finger across her lips.

Katie was having difficulty swallowing, she was having difficulty thinking. She placed her fork down and, lifting her plate, scraped the remains of the egg into the bin. Now she was having difficulty breathing. Her head was whirling and her body was behaving in a way it had never done before. Her desire for him was pulling at her, and she couldn't think straight. She wanted to feel his skin next to hers, feel his hands caressing her, have his mouth on hers.

She felt him come and stand behind her. His warm breath caressed the nape of her neck and he murmured something she couldn't understand in Portuguese. His hands untied the belt of her robe and she leaned against him as her robe fell open. Strangely she no longer felt shy. She felt nothing except longing and wonder that he was there with her. She felt no shame, no embarrassment. Just lust.

His hands were on her breasts and her breath caught in her throat.

She turned around in his arms and looked into his dark eyes.

'Take me to bed,' she whispered.

Lying in his arms felt so right. Everything about being with Fabio felt right. But she knew deep inside that for him, at least, this meant little. Why of all people did she have to go and fall for him? He'd made no secret of the fact that he intended to stay single.

She was getting ahead of herself. They both needed more time to get to know each other. Not that it would make any difference to the way she felt.

Outside the water was lapping gently, almost mimicking the rhythm of Fabio's heartbeat.

Katie squinted at her watch, which was illuminated by the harbour lights outside. Nine-thirty. Lucy could return any minute.

'Fabio, wake up,' Katie whispered.

He moaned in his sleep and his arm pulled her closer. Katie would have liked nothing better than to stay exactly where she was, possibly for the rest of her life, but she didn't want Lucy to look for her or Fabio and find them. Some things were better left private.

Propping herself on her elbow, she looked down at his face. In sleep he was more severe looking, but there was a vulnerability about him she'd seen once before. 'You need to get up, Fabio,' she whispered again.

His eyes flickered open, and as he came to and saw her he smiled and pulled her towards him.

'You're pretty special—you know that, don't you?'

His words should have given her a glow, but they didn't. She wanted to be more than pretty special. She wanted him to love her, the way she loved him. Nothing less would ever be enough.

'You're not bad yourself,' she replied lightly. She leaped out of bed and tossed him her robe. 'Now, scoot. I'm going to shower before Lucy arrives back.'

Katie sat by the side of Lucy's bed and brushed away a lock of hair that had fallen over the sleeping child's face. As she'd expected, Lucy had rushed into her room as soon as she'd returned, wanting to tell her all about the evening. It had taken Katie all her persuasive powers to coax the excited girl into bed after more than an hour had passed and Lucy had begun to look exhausted.

Katie was surprised at how fond she'd become of Lucy over the last few weeks. For a while after Richard's death she had thought she would never be able to feel anything ever again. That she would never let herself get close to anyone again, in case she lost them too. Yet here she was, and despite herself she'd allowed two people into her heart. How had she let that happen?

Fabio wasn't in it for the long term. He'd never pretended otherwise. But she was sure she meant more to him than just an affair. Sighing, she stood and looked out of the window. She didn't really know for sure, did she? She'd never met anyone like him before. He was used to having relationships that weren't serious. She wasn't. She thought back to what he'd told her about his family. It couldn't have been easy for him as a child. Shunted between two arguing parents who had put their own lives ahead of their child. No wonder he had such a downer on marriage and no wonder he didn't want children.

But marriage didn't have to be like that. Her parents had been deeply in love until the day they'd died. And take Suzy and Richard. If Richard had lived…she swallowed the familiar lump in her throat…there was no way those two would have ever separated. Fabio shouldn't let his own experiences cloud his view of marriage. As she turned away and tiptoed out of Lucy's room, a thought crept into her head. Could she change his mind?

CHAPTER TWELVE

THE next day, they set off to where Mark's race was due to start at two. Fabio had left with Mark before Amelia and Lucy had been up.

As Katie had known he would, Fabio had come to her when everyone was asleep. They had made love again, before she'd fallen asleep in his arms. When she woke up he'd gone. She hugged the memory of their night together, praying she hadn't given herself away to Mark by blushing furiously when she'd seen Fabio at breakfast.

Lucy could hardly sit still at the thought of seeing her father race.

'Mum says there's a special place for families to watch from. We can have ice cream—anything we want.' Katie and Amelia shared a smile. Despite being mature for her age, Lucy was still, at the end of the day, a little girl.

'And if he wins, he will be the champion!' Lucy

bounced on her seat. 'And he'll be able to come home with us, won't he, Mum?'

'He'll be able to come home whether he becomes champion or not,' Amelia agreed with a smile. 'But let's hope he wins.'

The race track was already crowded with spectators by the time they arrived. Someone met them at the entrance and escorted them upstairs to a small room with a balcony overlooking the race track. The sound of cars tuning up filtered through the window. A large flat-screen television rotated different views of the pits, where the crews and drivers were making last-minute preparations, as well of the track where the race would take place.

'At least it's not as loud up here,' Amelia said.

They were offered drinks and snacks and, to Lucy's delight, ice cream. They settled down to watch the TV screen. Not that it was very interesting. Just shots of helmeted and jumpsuited men working over sleek racing cars. But eventually the cars were lined up at the start of the race.

'That's my dad!' Lucy said excitedly, pointing to a blue car near the front.

'How do you know?' Katie asked. Apart from the colours, they all looked the same to her.

''Cos it has his number, silly.'

'The other blue one is his teammate,' Amelia said. 'I have to agree with you, Katie, they all look the same to me. I rely on the commentators to tell me where Mark is.'

'How many laps?' Katie asked.

'Fifty-eight. Do you want to watch the start from the balcony?'

Katie wondered what was keeping Fabio. He would miss the start of the race. Just then the images on the TV panned to the pit where Mark's crew were and Katie saw Fabio's dark head as he leaned in to hear what one of the pit team was saying. The sight of him sent her pulse thrumming as memories from the night before rushed back into her head. Not that she'd been able to stop thinking about him all day.

'Fabio's back. He must have decided to watch from down there,' she said, hoping she wasn't blushing again.

The cars started with a roar and after a warm up lap began to race in earnest, each one jostling for position. Katie caught her breath as a car passed the one in front seeming to miss it only by a whisker.

'It's hot. I think I'll go back inside,' Amelia said.

Katie stayed outside where she could enjoy the warmth.

Every few minutes a stream of cars would rush past. Having had enough of the sun, she was about to go back inside when the screech of a car in trouble caught her attention. Smoke was billowing from its engine as it careered across the track, forcing cars behind to swerve in order to miss it. Her breath caught as she noticed the colour. Blue. Was it Mark?

The driver fought hard to get the car under control, but as if it were all happening in slow motion, the car flipped several times before coming to rest the right way up against the barrier.

Feeling sick, Katie watched as men started to run towards the car. She felt even sicker as she recognised that Fabio was one of them. Was he crazy? Judging by the smoke coming from the engine, the car could explode anytime.

She was only dimly aware of Amelia and Lucy

standing next to her. Amelia had turned a ghastly white and looked as if she might faint.

'It's all right, Mummy,' Lucy was shouting, pulling at her mother's arm. 'It's not Daddy.'

Amelia sank into one of the armchairs. 'Thank God.'

Katie shared her relief, but Fabio! He was putting his life at risk. Feeling increasingly nauseous, she couldn't tear her eyes away as he ran to the injured driver and leaned right into the wrecked car. Right behind him were men running, carrying fire extinguishers. What if Fabio couldn't get the injured driver out before the car was engulfed in flames? She knew he would never leave the man to die.

He was tugging and gesticulating. The other men were beside him now, helping him. With the sheer numbers they managed to extract the driver and were running away from the car, carrying the injured driver between them.

Run, God damn it, Fabio. Run!

Then with a blinding flash the wrecked car exploded into a sheet of flame.

Smoke billowed into the air, obscuring Katie's vision. She was only dimly aware that the race had been stopped. Her heart was crashing against her ribs so violently she thought she would be sick.

Please. Not again. Don't do this to me again.

Then out of the smoke the four men appeared, still carrying their patient, and Katie recognised Fabio's dark head. He was all right! He was alive. Katie sank back onto the chair behind her, placed her head in her hands and sobbed.

'What am I going to do?' Katie wailed.

Suzy put her arm around Katie's shoulder. They had returned home the day after the race. Mark had gone on to win, and the injured driver was doing well in hospital with surprisingly few injuries, but Katie couldn't bring herself to join in the celebrations. She'd excused herself and, apart from doing Lucy's physio, had remained in her cabin all evening. She didn't want to see Fabio, not until she knew what she was going to do. He'd knocked on her cabin door late the night of the race, but she'd feigned sleep. She'd felt relieved when the next morning she'd heard that Fabio had been called away to see another patient somewhere in Europe and had left already.

'Oh, sweetie, you do have it bad, don't you?' Suzy said sympathetically. 'But what do you mean, what are you going to do?'

'I love him, and I wish I didn't.'

'You can't help who you fall in love with,' Suzy said. 'Why don't you see where it takes you? From what you tell me, he isn't immune to you either.'

Katie sniffed. 'He doesn't love me. Even if he did, he's wrong for me, wrong, wrong, wrong.'

'You don't know that. Men like him do change their ways. When they meet the right person.'

Katie blew her nose. 'It's not just that. He reminds me so much of Richard. Fabio doesn't seem to care whether he lives or dies, and I can't bear the thought of something happening to him.'

Suzy stiffened.

'I didn't mean that. Oh, Suzy, I'm sorry. Of course Richard wanted to live. He had you and Ricky. He wasn't like Fabio at all. Fabio puts his life at risk for fun. And Richard, he put his life at risk because he had no choice.'

'Let me get this straight. You love Fabio, but you think he doesn't love you. You're scared he's going to break your heart. You're also scared he's going to kill himself in some mad adventure, leaving you all alone.'

'That's about it. Pathetic, huh?'

'I don't think there's anything pathetic about loving someone so much you can't bear to live without them.' Suzy's eyes grew moist. 'But if I had my time all over again—even if I'd known when I met Richard that our time together would be limited—I would have still wanted to be with him. There would never have been a choice.' Suzy blew her nose. 'Fabio didn't go after the racing driver out of some idea that it would be fun, Katie. He did it because he felt he had no choice. Would you rather he was the kind of man who stood back and let others take the risks?'

'No—I mean yes.' Katie shook her head, feeling miserable. 'I don't know. All I do know is that I couldn't bear it if someone close to me died again. I'm not strong enough.'

'I think you are,' Suzy said quietly, and Katie was reminded of Fabio saying the same thing to her that night on the yacht.

'Anyway…' she attempted a smile '…I guess I'll get over him. I have no choice. I've no reason to think I'm anything more than a passing whim as far as he's concerned.'

'Maybe he cares for you more than you think.' At the sound of cries coming from the nursery Suzy got to her feet. 'Baby calling. Katie, why don't you talk to him? Tell him how you feel. I can't imagine that Fabio will put his life in danger to save people from burning cars every day of the week.'

'I know he won't. But there's all this other stuff he does. One way or another. it looks like he's determined to kill himself.' Katie followed Suzy into the nursery. 'When he hurt his ankle it was because he was BASE jumping. The article I read said someone had died recently doing exactly the kind of thing he does. This recklessness of his—it's in him and it's never going to go away.'

Suzy picked Ricky up from his cot. 'The item you read could be exaggerating.' She placed her small son down on his changing mat and peeled off his wet nappy. Once he was changed and redressed in his sleepsuit, Suzy sat down and started breastfeeding.

'And even if it isn't, Katie, you have to accept that's who Fabio is and you have to decide whether it is better to live with him in your life, knowing that you will always worry about him, or whether it is better to live without him and all the joy and yes, pain, that love can bring. Unfortunately, loving someone comes at a price. I for one think that price is worth paying.' Suzy's voice hitched as she looked down at her suckling child.

As Katie watched mother and son her heart squeezed. One day she would like to have children. But please, God, she would have the children's father safe at home beside her. And right now all of it seemed like no more than a far-fetched dream.

'Anyone fancy going to Ascot?' Jenny asked, waving tickets in the air as if she'd just won the Lottery. 'Give us all a chance to dress up.'

Katie was getting used to the fact that their patients would drop off tickets for almost any event that she could imagine. Most of the time she declined.

Fabio had gone from his patient in Europe to Brazil for a couple of weeks and so she hadn't seen him. She didn't know whether she was dismayed or relieved by his absence. She only knew she missed seeing him every day.

'I don't think I'll bother,' Rose said, patting her ever-increasing girth. 'All I want to do these days after work is change into my pyjamas and have an early night. I went last year, though, and it was fun. You should go, Katie. Take your sister-in-law if she would like to go.'

Katie took the tickets from Jenny. 'I wouldn't want to stop anyone else from going,' she said.

'They wouldn't let me in probably,' Jenny grinned. 'I don't do dresses. Anyway, horses bore me.'

'What about you, Vicki?' Katie asked the nurse who was writing up her notes at the desk. They weren't expecting any more patients and would be closing up soon.

'Can't. My husband is on duty that day. I've already checked. But he says if no one wants the tickets for the football game next Saturday, could he please have them?'

'They're his.' Jenny scrabbled around in a drawer before finding a bunch of tickets. 'And if anyone else wants to go, there's more where these came from.'

The footballers who Katie had been treating regularly dropped off tickets for their home matches. One of them kept asking her to go out with him, but she always refused. Maybe she should reconsider. The worst danger a footballer got themselves into was usually a sprained ankle or a torn Achilles' tendon. But she knew she never would go out with the footballer. The simple fact was he wasn't Fabio.

'I'll ask my sister-in-law if she fancies Ascot,' Katie said. 'Would it be okay if I let you know tomorrow?'

Jenny nodded. 'Take your time. Hey, does anyone know when Fabio is due back? Some of his patients have been phoning for appointments. Most are happy to see Jonathan if it's an emergency, but one or two are pretty adamant that only Fabio will do.'

Vicki looked up from her note-writing. 'Let me guess. The women.'

Jenny feigned innocence. 'Now, why would you say that?'

Katie forced a smile, even though it hurt her to think of Fabio with other women. He could have phoned her or texted her. Something. But he hadn't. Was he regretting sleeping with her? Even worse, now that he had, had he lost interest? Was she just another notch in his bedpost?

'He's due back tonight, so he'll be in tomorrow. I'm surprised he didn't let you know, Jenny. It's not like him.' Rose puckered her brow.

'Maybe he can't get a signal in Brazil.' Jenny sighed.

'Don't be a goose, Jenny,' Vicki said. 'Brazil isn't exactly Third World.'

Katie closed her ears to the rest of the chat. Her stomach was churning at the thought of seeing Fabio again and knowing that whatever had between them was over.

But wasn't that what she wanted? Hadn't she told herself that she would tell him that a relationship was impossible? She felt bruised and hurt that he hadn't given her the chance. It seemed that her fears had come true. It was one thing for her to decide she couldn't risk loving him, quite another for him to treat her as if she meant nothing. Could she bear to continue to work at the practice knowing she would see him almost every day for the foreseeable future and having to hear about his conquests, pretending she didn't love him?

Her heart slammed against her ribs. How could she have been so stupid as to fall in love with him? Now she knew that he didn't need to die to break her heart.

She was putting Ricky down for the night when the doorbell rang. Leaving Suzy to answer it, she carried on tucking her nephew in. He was growing so quickly. Before they knew it, he'd be toddling around.

'Katie, it's Fabio.' Suzy's voice came from behind her.

'Fabio!' Immediately her heart started racing. Had he come to tell her it was all over? Before they came face to face at work? Well, if he had, she wouldn't give herself away.

A glance in the mirror confirmed her worst fears. She looked as if she'd spent the night arguing with a hurricane. Her hair was all over the place, she had a smear of baby food on her cheek and she was wearing her oldest pair of tracksuit bottoms. Bloody typical.

Noticing her hesitation, Suzy gave her a small push. 'He's waiting,' she hissed.

'I can't see him like this,' Katie hissed back. 'Can't you stall him?'

'What am I supposed to say? Could you wait half an hour while Katie dolls herself up for you?'

'I don't care what you tell him, just give me ten minutes—or fifteen,' she added when Suzy raised a sarcastic eyebrow.

'Can I help?' An amused voice came from the doorway.

Katie swung around with a little yelp. She had been so busy arguing with Suzy she hadn't heard him approach. Her nerves thrummed at the sight of him. He was just so damn sexy. And dear.

'It's okay. I was just putting Ricky down, but he's sleeping now.' She made a futile attempt to push her straggly hair behind her ear. 'Would you like a coffee? I was about to make one for myself.' Actually, she hadn't been. She simply couldn't think of anything to say.

'I wondered if you'd like to come out for dinner,' Fabio asked. 'I did try your mobile, but I couldn't get through.'

'Battery must be flat.'

Fabio seemed uncharacteristically nervous. No doubt this was where he gave her the boot. Of course he couldn't say anything in front of Suzy.

'About dinner?' If he'd noticed that dinner was the last thing she was ready for, he gave no sign of it.

'Tell you what, guys,' Suzy interrupted. 'Why don't I leave you two alone? There's a casserole in the oven you could have and I'm overdue a visit to my folks. Would it be all right if I left Ricky? I don't want to wake him.'

'Sure,' Katie said. She didn't know which was worse. Being alone here with Fabio or being in a restaurant.

'Home cooking sounds good to me,' Fabio said. 'If you're sure? I don't want to chase you out of your home.'

Suzy picked up her handbag and started putting on her coat. 'Honestly, I could do with a change of scenery. I've got my mobile, Katie, if you need me,' And with a last wave she was out of the door, leaving Katie facing Fabio.

'I should go and change,' Katie said. 'I don't suppose you could give me a few minutes?'

'You look perfect the way you are.' He stepped

towards her. 'Even the crusty baby food suits you.' He licked his finger and rubbed at her cheek. Her skin sizzled where he'd touched her.

'Now I'm definitely having a shower.' If he was going to tell her that sleeping with her had been a mistake, at least she wanted to feel less at a disadvantage. 'Could you listen out for Ricky for me?' She picked up a pile of magazines and shoved them at Fabio. 'Something to read while you wait.'

Fabio's mouth twitched. '*Cosmopolitan*? *Mother and Baby*? Not my usual reading material.' Then his eye caught one of the feature headlines— 'How to please your man'—and his smile widened. 'This one sounds interesting.' He shooed her away. 'Go. I'll be fine.'

When Katie emerged from the shower, Fabio was walking up and down with a crying Ricky on his shoulder. Katie hadn't heard the baby above the noise of the shower.

She went to take him from Fabio but he shook his head. 'He's settling,' he said quietly.

Katie went into the kitchen and set plates out,

checking on the casserole. It had another twenty minutes to go.

Back in the sitting room, Fabio was still pacing, with Ricky draped over his shoulder. Katie scooted around to his back to check that Ricky was asleep, only to be met with the solemn, wide-awake but content eyes of her nephew.

'Every time I try to put him back in his cot, or stop pacing, he starts crying again,' Fabio said. 'I think it's safer just to leave him where he is for the time being.'

Katie smothered a smile. Ricky had left a trail of regurgitated milk down the back of Fabio's shirt. This time it was his turn to look less than immaculate. She peered at him. Something was different. He was growing a beard or something. Well, not exactly a beard. More like six o'clock shadow. Whatever it was, it suited him. He had never seemed more sexy to Katie than now, with baby vomit and a couple of days' stubble on his face.

'I could always walk alongside you and feed you mouthfuls of casserole if you're hungry,' Katie offered.

Fabio grinned and her heart flipped, then his

expression turned serious. 'I'm not very hungry,' he said. 'But I thought we should talk.'

A shiver of apprehension ran up Katie's spine. This was it. The part where he told her it had all been a mistake and for the sake of their working relationship, could they just be friends? She steeled herself to pretend she felt the same.

'The thing is, Katie. I think I'm falling in love with you.'

It was as if a string orchestra had set up home inside her chest. He was falling in love with her!

'But it's not going to work,' he added quickly

Her heart plummeted. She knew now without a shadow of doubt that although she had told herself many times he wasn't the man for her, it was too late. Her heart had betrayed her. Reckless and a womaniser he may be, but she loved him. She would rather risk her heart with this man than spend her life safe but without him.

'And I think you care about me too,' Fabio said, his eyes searching hers.

'Really?' she prevaricated. 'What makes you say that?' If she was going to get the brush-off then she was going to damn well hang onto some dignity.

His smile was sad. 'Oh, Katie, do you really think you can hide your feelings? It is the thing I love about you the most. The way you can't pretend to be anything except who you are. Being with you is like being in a harbour. A place of safety from the storm.'

'So why can't we be together?' Katie sank down on the nearest armchair as Fabio continued to pace.

'For all sorts of reasons. First, I'm not the marrying kind. I don't believe that two people can live together without tearing each other apart.'

Marriage! Did he say marriage? Her mouth went dry.

'Who said anything about getting married? Don't you think you're jumping the gun a bit?'

'I'm just trying to be honest. I need you to know that wherever this goes, it can't be permanent.'

'Why? Why do you say that?'

He smiled, but there was no humour in his eyes. 'I saw the way my parents almost destroyed each other. They were in love once, they must have been. I was very young when they separated, but I still remember the fights.'

'Lots of couples make it. Your parents had

different stresses. It couldn't have been easy for them to follow careers that took them to opposite parts of the world.'

Fabio stopped pacing and looked at her. 'I know my parents weren't like everyone else's.' He started pacing again. 'Like many in his line, my father lived life too fast. Do you know what I'm saying?'

Katie shook her head, bewildered. 'I think you're going to have to spell it out.'

'My father took drugs and drank himself to an early grave. I watched him destroy himself. I swore then that I would never find my thrills in the bottom of a bottle or in chemicals. That's why I surf and take risks. It's the way I get my highs.' He paused. 'At least, it used to be. These days I get more of a buzz being with you.'

Katie's heart did a little dance and then fell over. He loved her, but he couldn't be with her.

Ricky whimpered and Fabio started pacing again. 'I know that marriages can break down, and that my parents had more pressure than most. God knows, I see enough of it every day, but that's not the only reason we can't be together.'

Katie's head was beginning to ache. If only Fabio would stop walking up and down.

'Go on,' she said quietly, knowing that whatever he had to say, she needed to hear it.

'My folks were so caught up in their own lives that when I got mumps as a child they didn't even notice. They left me with the housekeeper while they went away for the weekend.'

He took a deep breath, 'To be fair, they didn't know how sick I was going to get. They thought it was a simple case of mumps. Naturally it hadn't occurred to either of them to get me vaccinated.'

'Was this when you were in hospital? When you decided to become a doctor?'

He smiled. 'You remembered.'

As if she'd forget anything he'd ever told her.

'That came later,' he said. 'At first I was too sick to know where I was. All I remember is wanting my mother, and she wasn't there.' His voice thickened. 'I'm not telling you this, Katie, because I want your sympathy. I just need you to understand.'

When Fabio turned round, Katie saw that finally Ricky had fallen asleep. Gently she lifted him from Fabio and, going to the nursery, placed the baby back in his cot. When she returned to the sitting room, Fabio was staring into space. She had never seen him like this and her heart ached for him. She crossed over to his chair and, sitting on the floor, placed her head on his lap. His hand came out to stroke her hair.

'What happened while you were in hospital?' Katie asked, knowing Fabio hadn't reached the end of his story.

'Most kids who get mumps only get mild symptoms. I was one of the unlucky ones. For a while the nurses thought they were going to lose me. This time my mother did come. And my father. I have a vague recollection of them both sitting by my bed. I was happy. I thought it meant that they were going to get back together. If getting sick meant I would live with both my parents, then I was glad.' He sighed heavily. 'But as I got better, they started arguing again. Each blaming the other for my illness. The nurses had even to evict them at one point. Not exactly what a child wants to happen.'

His hands stilled in her hair. 'I got better, obviously, and I think I grew up then. I decided I would never rely on anyone again. It's also when

I decided to become a doctor. I saw it as a way out. It gave me hope that I could lead a life far removed from that of my parents. You asked me if I ever wanted to be a singer or an actor—believe me, there was nothing I wanted to do less.

'When I got better I returned to boarding school. Most people hated it there, but I liked it. There was no shouting, no arguments, and if there wasn't love either, that was better than the pain I felt living with my parents. I learned how to depend only on myself.'

'So now you know how not to be with your children. You would be a very different parent from what they were, I think. You'd have to stop taking risks, or at least not as many, but perhaps it would be worth it.'

His hands gripped her shoulders briefly, before they dropped to his sides. 'Katie, how simply you see life. Living with me would destroy that. I would end up tearing you in two. I can't change and you want me to. Despite what I told you about my parents, I will never be the pipe-and-slippers type.'

Katie scrambled to her feet, feeling a warm tide

of anger wash over her. Placing her hands on her hips, she turned to face him.

'I'm sorry, Fabio, but all this sounds like so much hogwash to me. An excuse why you can't try and have a loving, committed relationship. If it can't be with me, that's one thing, but pay me the respect I deserve, and don't lie to me.'

He looked up at her with such an expression of regret and sadness it took her breath away.

'Tell me, Katie, do you want children in your life?'

The question took her by surprise. 'I always did. Growing up with only Richard, I always wanted to be part of a big family one day. It scares me sometimes now, especially when I think of Lucy and Richard, and know that I will go through my life terrified that something will happen to my child. But now you ask, I guess it is a fear I'm prepared to live with. I would just need their father to tell me when I was being over-protective.'

'I thought so,' Fabio said slowly. 'Anyone who sees you with children knows that you are meant to have them. Three or four, perhaps.'

'Hey, I'm only coming to terms with the fact I

might have them one day, I'm not planning to get pregnant any time soon.' She tried to keep her tone light, but her voice came out with a wobble. The feeling of dread was getting stronger.

'And that's the problem. It's not just that I'd be a hopeless risk as husband material, I can't have children, Katie. The mumps I had as a child left me sterile.'

CHAPTER THIRTEEN

'How can you be sure?' Katie's head was spinning.

'When I was eighteen a girl I slept with told me she was pregnant. As you can imagine, I was stunned. I saw my life going up in smoke. When I told my mother, it was the first and last time I had gone to her for advice, or financial support for the girl at least, she told me that she didn't think it could be mine. Then she explained about the mumps.

'In some ways, although I wasn't ready to become a father, I was devastated. I had become used to the idea that there was going to be a child in this world who had my genes and I knew that I wasn't going to be like my parents and put my own needs first.

'I didn't believe my mother. I suspected she just wanted me to get out of having a responsibility for the child, in the same way she'd abandoned her responsibility, so I decided to get my fertility checked.' His mouth twisted in a parody of a smile. 'As you can imagine, it took a bit of nerve for an eighteen-year-old to put himself through what I had to do. Donating a specimen in a room, knowing that there were people almost right outside, wasn't exactly conducive to producing the specimen.'

He rubbed a hand across his cheek. 'Turns out that my mother was right. My sperm count was so low as to be almost negligible.'

'I'm sorry, Fabio. That must have been hard.'

'It wasn't so hard at the time. In a way I was almost relieved. At least I knew the child couldn't be mine, and when I challenged the girl, she admitted there was no baby. It was all a bit of a con to try and extract money from my family.'

'And now?'

His smile was ghostly. 'I got used to not being able to have children. I didn't see the point in marrying. So it didn't matter. Until now.'

He stopped his pacing and came to crouch at her feet. 'I thought it was only fair to tell you.'

Katie reached out and brushed a lock of hair from his eyes.

'Thank you for telling me,' she said, 'but there are other ways to have children, you know. Besides, I don't care. I love you. You're enough for me. Can't you see that?'

He took her hand and placed it back in her lap. 'But for how long, Katie? We can't take the risk that one day you'll want more. *You* can't take that risk. I won't let you.'

The blood in Katie's veins turned to ice. She couldn't accept what he was telling her. Wasn't her love enough for him? It should be. He was enough for her.

Fabio sighed heavily. 'One thing I have done is to make my peace with my mother—and my childhood. And while I was in Brazil I got to thinking about the kids who don't have parents. So I've set in motion a project to build a home for these kids, one where they'll get love as well as the best education money can buy. My father left me a lot of money, but I never wanted to touch it. I think he would be pleased that the money he left and the money his estate still makes through royalties will be used to do some good. So, at least if I can't have children of my own, I'm making a difference to some child's life. I have you to thank for that, Katie. Somewhere along the way, you've made me believe I can be a better man.'

'You were always a good man, Fabio, you just didn't know it,' Katie said.

Fabio half smiled. 'If I were a good man, I would have never let you love me. The only thing left for me to do is set you free.'

After the door closed behind Fabio, Katie sat deep in thought.

What would it be like to know that children were never going to be part of her future? Because if she and Fabio did find a way to be together, that was what life would be like.

She stood and crossed over to the window. A car passed in the otherwise deserted street.

Did it matter? A life without children if she had Fabio? Of course it did, but, as she'd told him, she would rather a life with him than without. And there was the project he'd spoken about. Those children would always be part of their lives.

There was adoption too, of course. That would be a possibility. But the feeling of unease she'd had since they'd spoken wouldn't go away. Why was he telling her this? Was it just an easy way out of a relationship he didn't wish to pursue? She shook her head. She couldn't believe Fabio would be so cowardly.

He had no right to decide what she could or couldn't cope with. Although the thought of never having children of her own saddened her, she knew that she could never walk away. All she had to do now was make him see sense.

Fabio studied the nervous man sitting opposite him. Luke, the son of a famous TV presenter, had asked specifically for Fabio when he'd made his appointment.

After spending a few minutes on small talk, Fabio decided it was time to get to the bottom of whatever was bothering this otherwise fit and healthy-looking specimen in front of him.

'Would you like to tell me why you're here?' he asked.

A deep red washed up Luke's neck and face.

'Whatever it is, Luke, you can tell me. I promise you, there's nothing I haven't seen or heard since I qualified as a doctor.'

'My girlfriend and I were—um—having sex

last night when she felt something that didn't seem right.'

'In your testicles?' Fabio guessed.

Luke nodded miserably. 'Is it cancer?' he said.

'We won't know until I've had a look and done some tests. Why don't you get up on the couch so I can have a look?'

Luke did as he was told. As soon as he'd felt the lump Fabio knew instantly it would require further investigation.

'It could be a cyst,' he told Luke, 'but we won't know until we do an ultrasound at the hospital. I have to be honest with you, though, it feels a little too solid to be a cyst.'

'I'm supposed to be getting married in three months,' Luke said as he pulled his trousers up. 'What if it is cancer? What then? Will we be able to go through with the wedding? What about children? God, this is such a shock. Could I die?'

'If you have testicular cancer,' Fabio said, 'and at this stage it's only an if, and we've caught it early, then there's a good chance that you will be okay. You may need chemotherapy and you will have to have an orchidectomy—that's a procedure to remove the affected testicle—but it will be straightforward. One thing you will have to consider is whether to have your sperm stored before treatment. Unfortunately the chemo does tend to make you infertile, but if you freeze sperm it gives you an excellent chance of having children later on once the treatment is over.'

He waited until Luke was sitting down again. 'I know there's a lot to take in and you'll want to talk it over with your fiancée, but I need to get you seen at the hospital as soon as possible. Luckily my colleague, Dr Cavendish, works there. I'll give him a ring and see if he can squeeze you in this afternoon.'

Luke was pale now. 'Won't it look horrible—disgusting, even—if they remove one of my testicles? What if it puts my fiancée off? What if she decides she doesn't want to marry someone who is half a man? Could I even blame her?'

Fabio went round to Luke's side of the desk and squeezed his shoulder. 'She'll hardly notice, I promise. They reconstruct the testicle after surgery so it looks almost as it did before. And if she loves you, and seeing that she's agreed to marry you, it seems she does, she'll just be glad to have you fit and well again.'

'She agreed to marry me before she knew I was sick. It's not fair to keep her to her promise now, especially if I get sicker.' He stood up. 'Thank you for seeing me, Doctor,' he said heavily.

Luke seemed so dazed and frightened that Fabio's heart went out to him.

'Look, take a seat in the waiting room,' he said, 'while I make some calls. If they can see you this afternoon, and if I can clear my diary, I'll come with you to the hospital. That way we can discuss your options as soon as we know what exactly it is we're dealing with.'

For the first time since Luke had entered Fabio's consulting room, he looked relieved. 'Would you, Doc? I can't tell you how much it would mean to me. That way I don't need to call Clarissa until I'm sure what I want to tell her.'

'Take a seat outside. I'll be out shortly.'

Five minutes later Fabio replaced the receiver and leaned back in his chair. He had managed to arrange an appointment for Luke that afternoon. They would do an ultrasound first to rule out a cyst and then they would take it from there. All that remained was for Fabio to clear his diary so he could be with Luke when he got the diagnosis—good or bad.

His mind went back to the day he'd found out he couldn't have children. His mother had been away filming, so he had phoned Kendrick. It was always Kendrick he turned to when he was in trouble. They'd been at boarding school together and had got into mischief together and were closer than most brothers. Kendrick had been due to leave for America that afternoon but had changed his flight immediately.

'Can't let you go through this on your own,' he'd said.

Kendrick was the only person who knew what it had been like for Fabio, growing up without his parents being around. His mother and Fabio's father had been brother and sister, but where Fabio's father had little interest in anyone except those directly involved in the music world, Kendrick's father was overbearing and controlling. It was hardly surprising Kendrick had managed to get drummed out of the army. As far as Fabio knew, his uncle rarely spoke to his son.

When Fabio had been told that his sperm count was so low as to make the chances of having children almost impossible, Kendrick had called for him and then they had gone out and for the first and only time in his life Fabio had got plastered, along with his cousin.

So Fabio knew what Luke was going through. How much worse for Luke that he was engaged to someone who expected that they would have children. But as he'd told his frightened patient, even if he turned out to have testicular cancer, and Fabio was pretty sure that would be the case, at least there were other options. Children could still be part of his future.

And maybe they could be part of his. He hadn't been able to stop thinking of Katie's face since he'd spoken to her. Maybe he was being a coward, refusing to face life, whatever it brought? In that way, Katie was far braver than he was.

CHAPTER FOURTEEN

AS HE'D promised, Fabio accompanied Luke to the hospital. It was just as well he did, because he was sure that Luke would have crashed had he driven himself.

'Isn't this going beyond the call of duty?' Luke said. 'I mean, you can't go with your patients to hospital every time, can you?'

'It's all part of the service, although…' Fabio hesitated. 'I like to pop in every now and again anyway to keep in touch with the staff, so don't worry. If it makes you feel any better, it's not just for you.' But that wasn't the whole truth. As he'd been talking to Luke an idea had formed in his head. If Luke was going to see the fertility specialist about storing sperm, perhaps Fabio should have a word too. Sometimes, not often admittedly, sperm counts improved over time and there was always that small possibility that his had. He thought back to what Katie had said about getting on with life. She was right. At the very least he would have his infertility confirmed. Knowing kids were out of the question might make his decision to keep away from Katie easier. It was bloody hard. Every time he saw her, he wanted to pull her into his arms and when he wasn't with her, she was always in his mind. He could barely sleep these days for thinking of her. Hell, even big wave surfing had lost its charm.

At the hospital, he left Luke in the capable hands of the surgeon Jonathan had arranged for him to see. He had an hour or so before Luke would have his diagnosis.

Feeling a little like a thief, he found his way to the fertility clinic. He referred patients there fairly regularly and so knew the doctor who ran the clinic.

'Fabio! Good to see you. Have you come to check up on us?' Dr Aubrey was in her fifties with penetrating blue eyes and a ready smile.

'Not exactly. Look, is there somewhere we can go to talk?' he asked.

Dr Aubrey frowned. 'Sure. Come this way.'

When they were settled and had finished discussing the possibility of Luke storing sperm,

which as Fabio suspected would be straightforward, Fabio cleared his throat.

'I wanted to ask you whether you'd do a sperm
analysis on me,' he said.

'Not a problem. You know the procedure?'

When Fabio nodded, Dr Aubrey went on. 'I
could do with a little medical history, Fabio. It
will help the embryologists.'

'Mumps when I was a child. Had a sperm
analysis when I was eighteen Very low motility.
So low as to make the chances of conceiving
almost negligible.'

Dr Aubrey placed the fingertips of her hands
together and tapped them together gently.

'That was, what? Ten years ago?'

'About then.'

'We've come a long way since then. It's certainly worth getting it checked out. Even if there
are one or two motile sperm, we could use them
to achieve a pregnancy using ICSI.'

'I've been reading about it. I didn't think too
much about it…until now.'

'You've met someone and now children seem
less like a crazy idea. Am I right?'

Fabio managed a smile. 'That's about it.'

'Okay. You can do it now if you have time. Or would you prefer to do it at home and bring it in first thing? You know it has to be with us within an hour of production, but we can give you everything you need.'

Riding ten-metre waves had never felt quite this terrifying.

'Home, I think.'

'Okay let's get you the pack. It has all the information you need on it. Hand it in tomorrow morning and we should have the results by the afternoon.' Dr Aubrey held out her hand. 'Good luck.'

After leaving his pack for the morning in his car, Fabio returned to the outpatient clinic to track down Luke.

He was just in time to see him emerging from the surgeon's office looking distraught and shocked. 'It's definitely cancer. But luckily it's early stage and there's time for me to deposit some sperm before I have to start treatment. They're going to do some procedure—an orchid—something early next week.'

'An orchidectomy,' Fabio filled in. 'They remove the testicle.'

'Then they're going to start with chemotherapy. They say that there's a good chance I will be sterile after that so, as you said, they advise storing as much sperm as I can before treatment starts.'

Luke sank down on a chair. 'I still can't believe this is happening to me.'

Fabio sat down next to him. 'Life can be awful sometimes. But you can store your sperm for years—until you're ready to have children. You might not even have to have IVF either. They could use it to do IUI.' Seeing that Luke was looking bewildered he added, 'Intra-uterine insemination. It's where they kind of squirt the sperm straight into the uterus at the appropriate time in your partner's cycle.'

'I don't know what to say to her. I don't know what I should do. Maybe I should walk away and let her get on with her life. Why should she be saddled with someone sick? She's young. It isn't fair. I love her too much to put her through all that.'

'And she loves you enough to want to go through it with you. If you leave her now, if you exclude her from everything—your life, your illness—she'll be hurt. You have to at least talk to her. Tell her what's going on in your head. You might be surprised to hear what she has to say.' As he said the words, Fabio knew he wasn't just speaking about Luke, he was talking about himself. One way or another, he and Katie had a whole lot of talking to do.

Fabio delivered his specimen the next morning on his way to work. Then he set off in the opposite direction to see Lucy. Amelia had phoned him to say that the little girl was wheezier than usual and she was worried, so would he mind calling in? He'd suggested that she call Katie and ask her to come out too. The thought of Katie made him feel warm. Being with her felt good. Everything about her felt good. More than good. When he was with her it was as if he'd come home. If, and he knew this was a long shot, the sperm sample he had delivered showed that there was a chance he could father children, then there was no reason why he and Katie couldn't be together. Up until he had fallen in love with her, he'd thought that he would never trust enough to commit to marriage but he knew deep down that Katie would never let him down. Not even if her life depended on it. On the other hand, if, as was likely, the results of his specimen test came back negative, he would walk away from her. He loved her that much.

Amelia met him at the door, her eyes shadowed with anxiety. 'Lucy doesn't sound good,' she said. 'Katie's here and is giving her some physio to help clear the secretions from her lungs.'

Fabio hugged Amelia. 'I'll go up and see her straight away.' He knew better than to offer Amelia false reassurances. She knew almost as much about her daughter's illness as most experts.

Upstairs, Katie was just tucking Lucy into bed. Although, along with her nebuliser, she had her computer games in her lap, she was making no attempt to play with her game. Even from the doorway Fabio could hear her rasping breaths. He was immediately alarmed.

'Hey, Luce,' he said, careful to keep his voice level and his face expressionless. 'Mum says you're not feeling too good.'

He could see his concern reflected in Katie's eyes. He'd seen Lucy a couple of days ago and her chest had been fine then. But that was the nature of this illness.

'My chest feels tight. It's a little better since Katie gave me a long session of physio.' She looked at him with tears in her eyes. He couldn't recall seeing Lucy cry before and it alarmed him even more than her breathing. 'I won't have to go into hospital, will I? I don't want to. I want to stay here.'

'I'll have to examine you, Luce, before I can make a decision about what we're going to do, you know that, but if we can keep you at home, we will.' He took his stethoscope out of his medical bag. 'Could you lift your PJs while I have a listen to your chest?'

He wasn't surprised to hear crackles. There was no doubt Lucy had a chest infection. He checked her pulse and respirations. Not as high as he'd feared. 'Tell you what. I'm going to give you mucolytic through your nebuliser and some antibiotics. I'll come back to see you this evening and assess how you're doing. If there's an improvement, then fine, you can stay at home; if not, I may have to admit you to hospital.' He lifted her chin, cutting off her protests and forcing her to look into his eyes. 'You trust me, don't you?'

Lucy nodded, her mouth trembling.

'Okay, then. We'll get you sorted for the time being. We'll decide what to do later. If that's okay with Mum?'

Amelia nodded too.

'You can get me on my mobile if you're at all worried,' he said. 'And I'll come running. That's a promise.'

Mother and daughter seemed reassured. In many ways Fabio would have liked to have taken the easy way out and admitted Lucy to hospital, but the easy way out for the doctor wasn't always what was best for the child.

Leaving Amelia with Lucy, he took Katie aside.

'Are you comfortable with what I'm proposing?' he asked. 'You have as much say in this as the rest of us.'

Katie looked at him with her clear grey eyes. 'Hospitals aren't always the best places for children. She's scared to death of going there. I think I'll hang about here for the rest of the afternoon and give her some more physio.'

Despite the reassurances Fabio had given mother and daughter, he was relieved that Katie would be on hand. She would see any change and get in touch with him immediately.

'Don't you have somewhere else to be?' he asked.

'I did,' she said softly, 'but right now it's Lucy who needs me most.'

There was something in her expression that made him pause. But she pushed him gently towards the door. 'I know you're on call for the practice today, so get going. I'll call you if I need you.'

He looked at her one final time. He wished that was true.

With a heavy heart Katie watched Fabio's car pull away. She did have somewhere she should go. Somewhere important, but if she'd told him, he might have changed his mind about watching Lucy at home for a bit. Today was the day that Suzy had been invited to Buckingham Palace to collect the medal for Richard on his behalf. Suzy's mum and dad were going too, and Suzy also wanted Katie to be there.

Still, it couldn't be helped. As she'd told Fabio, it was the living that mattered. Loving Fabio had made her believe that and, besides, Suzy would have her parents. But today would have been a final goodbye to Richard, not that she would ever stop grieving for him.

She made her way back upstairs. If only things could have been different between her and Fabio, she could have found comfort in his arms today when she needed it most. Her heart ached as she recalled the words she'd said to him. *I'll call you if I need you.* And so she would. For a patient, but never, it seemed, for herself.

Fabio felt distinctly unsettled all day as he saw the patients who swore they couldn't go another day without seeing him. It was mainly sore throats, colds and the odd request for sleeping and slimming pills. The last two he always turned down so you'd think word might have got around by now. He had a letter from Luke's surgeon on his desk and his surgery was scheduled for the end of the week in order to give him time to produce three samples to be frozen. Luke had phoned him to say that he had talked to his fiancée and she was adamant that nothing, not even the possibility of never having children, would come between them and that he was relieved and feeling more optimistic about the future.

There was a tap on the door and Rose stuck her head around. 'Finished for the day?'

'Apart from one or two home visits.' He explained about Lucy and that he had left Katie keeping an eye on things until he was able to pop back.

'Katie?' Rose frowned. 'Katie is with Lucy? But she's off duty.'

'I know, but apparently Amelia phoned her after phoning me. They've come to rely on her a lot.'

Rose was still frowning. 'But she'll miss the medal ceremony.'

'Medal ceremony? What medal ceremony?' It was the first he'd heard about it.

'The one for her brother. He's been awarded a Conspicuous Gallantry Cross. The presentation is at the palace this afternoon.'

Fabio was stunned. Katie had given up her afternoon, and not just any afternoon, so that she could help Lucy and her family. Her unselfish behaviour made him feel small. How often had he put the needs of others before his own? And wasn't that what he was doing, seeking her out when he knew he had nothing to offer her?

'She can't miss the ceremony,' he said, getting to his feet. He looked at his watch. Two o'clock. 'What time did you say it was due to start?'

'About four. I think there's tea in the garden or something beforehand.'

'Look, Rose. I know you have enough on your plate at the moment, being pregnant and due to deliver almost any day, but could you do me a favour?'

'Whatever you want.'

'Could you ring the lab and get me Lucy's results?'

'No problem. Anything else?'

Fabio hesitated. 'I'm going to collect Katie from Lucy's house—she'll need a dress or something for the palace. Could you help me pick one out? And then could you stay with Lucy and Amelia until I get back there? I'll drop you off, see how she's doing, take Katie to the medal ceremony and then drop back in on them on the way back.'

Rose was already on her way out of the door. 'I gather her invitation was for her plus one, so you could stay.' She paused. 'She might need a shoulder to lean on, and I'm guessing the shoulder she needs is right in front of me.'

Fabio's phone was ringing but he ignored it. 'Would you ask Jenny to field my calls? Perhaps Jonathan could pick up any patients who need seeing.' He stopped. 'I owe you both. Meet me outside. I'll bring the car round.'

Rose was waiting outside the clinic and jumped into the car as Fabio screeched to a halt.

'The results for Lucy show a slightly elevated white count and CRP but nothing to cause concern. I can organise another blood sample while I'm there if you like.'

'Did I ever tell you that I love you, Rose?'

Rose smiled. 'You did once—at my wedding, if you remember.'

Fabio pointed his car in the direction of Katie's flat and pressed his foot to the accelerator. Too bad if he got a speeding ticket.

'A Dr Aubrey called to speak to you. I asked if it was urgent and she said no, but you should ring her at home when you got a chance.' She passed Fabio a slip of paper with a number. 'Nothing I can do, is there?'

He shook his head. 'Not right now. Maybe later.'

'You're in love with Katie. Aren't you?'

Fabio didn't bother to pretend. He knew Rose would see right through him.

'Yes,' he said simply.

'So what are you going to do about it?'

'I don't know. All I know is that making her happy is the most important thing in the world to me and if I can't do that, she's better off without me.'

Rose touched his hand lightly. 'Why is it you men think you know what is best for us?'

'You can talk,' Fabio retorted. 'Didn't you think you knew what was best for Jonathan when you kept your illness secret?'

'Touché. Are you telling me you have something wrong with you?' Her voice was anxious. 'Because even if you don't want to tell Katie, and I think you should, you should tell me, or Jonathan. Especially if it's something that might affect the practice.'

Fabio smiled grimly. 'I promise it's nothing that will affect my ability to see and treat patients.' He took a deep breath. Maybe it was time he shared his conflicted feelings with someone else. And who better than this woman, the wife of his friend, who had been through so much herself?

'I'm infertile. At least, I'm ninety-nine per cent sure I am.' The tyres screeched as he turned a corner. 'Sorry!'

'I think Katie would prefer to have you arrive in one piece than not at all,' Rose remonstrated. 'Have you told her about your infertility? Wait a minute! Dr Aubrey—is that why she was phoning?'

Fabio slowed the car to a reasonable speed. Killing Rose or injuring an innocent driver was not going to help matters. Jonathan, for all his laid-back manner, would take him apart piece by piece if anything happened to his beloved wife.

'Yes. I decided to have a sperm test so I can be sure.'

'Have you told Katie about this?'

'Some of it. I don't want her marrying someone who can't give her children.'

'So you want to marry her.'

'More than anything in this world. She makes me...feel complete.' He felt a bit of an idiot saying the words but it was true. Without Katie he'd never be completely whole.

'You should tell her,' Rose said. 'At least she'll know you love her.'

Fabio brought the car to a halt in front of Suzy's house. 'What? Like you did with Jonathan? From what he told me, that's why you ran away from him. Because you thought you were going to die. And it's partly why you had the operation. So you could give him children.'

'You two have been talking! But it wasn't as simple as that. C'mon. Let's grab something for Katie to wear.'

Fabio slapped his hand against his forehead. 'I haven't been thinking straight. How are we supposed to get in?'

But Rose just smiled and got out of the car. She walked over to a plant pot and lifted it. 'Ahah! One key!' She held it up for Fabio to see. 'She told me one day that she left a spare there. Said she was always managing to lock herself out. I did warn her it was the first place a thief would look, but she wouldn't listen. Seems your luck is changing.'

When they let themselves into the sitting room

Fabio saw an outfit was draped over the back of the sofa with a pair of matching shoes placed neatly next to it. Fabio recognised the dress at once. It was the one she had worn that night on board the yacht. The night when he had truly seen her for the first time. It was perfect.

'There's a handbag too. Looks like she had it all laid out ready.' Rose smiled. 'OK, lover boy, let's get going.'

Once again Fabio drove as fast as he could without risking crashing the car. It was almost four o'clock. They had thirty minutes to persuade Katie she had to go, get her into her outfit and get to the palace. Given the London traffic it would be close. Amelia answered the door looking far happier than she'd looked that morning.

'Fabio, I didn't expect you back until later.' Her eyes creased with anxiety. 'Is there anything wrong? Are the blood results bad?'

'Don't worry, Amelia, nothing's wrong. The blood results are fine. Honestly!' Amelia peered behind him, noticing Rose for the first time.

'Rose! What brings you here? Now I'm really worried.'

Quickly Rose explained why they'd come.

Amelia was immediately contrite. 'Katie never breathed a word. Of course she must go!'

'The trouble is,' Fabio said, glancing at his watch again, 'I don't think we're going to make it.'

'You leave getting there to Rose and I. Mark and I owe you both so much, do you think we're going to let Katie miss this?'

Fabio left Rose and Amelia conspiring and ran up the stairs to Lucy's bedroom. Katie and Lucy were reading a book together and Fabio was relieved that the little girl's breathing was back to being as close to normal as it ever was.

'Hi, Luce. Feeling better?' When Lucy nodded he took a surprised Katie by the hand. 'I just need to borrow Katie for a few hours. Is that okay? Rose is here and she'll stay with you until I get back.'

'Rose? Here?' Katie let Fabio pull her outside the room before turning to him. 'I think you should tell me what's going on. Has something happened? God, I can see by your face it has. What is it? Suzy? Ricky? For God's sake, Fabio, tell me.'

'Why didn't you tell me your brother was being awarded a posthumous medal this afternoon?'

Katie's face registered shock. 'How did you know?'

'Rose told me. *Vamos!* We have half an hour to get you there.' He started leading her down the stairs, but Katie literally dug her heels in. 'I'm not going. I'm staying right here. Who do you think you are to tell me what I should do? You have no right.'

'I have more right than you think, woman,' he growled. 'We haven't got time to argue.'

Still looking mystified, Katie let him lead her down the stairs. 'But I haven't got anything to wear. There's no way I can turn up at the palace like this.' She indicated her work top and matching trousers. 'They'll throw me out.'

'We have clothes—and shoes and handbag. Downstairs.' As they reached the foot of the stirs Rose silently handed Katie the clothes they had taken from Suzy's house.

'How did you get these?'

'Key. Flowerpot.' Rose gave her a gentle shove. 'Go on, Amelia will show you where to get changed.'

'But there's no time,' Katie wailed. 'I was supposed to be there no later than four.'

'Mark has our helicopter and a pilot standing by,' Amelia said. 'It will take five minutes, and Jonathan's used his contacts to clear a landing space close to the palace. Now, c'mon.'

'Or do I have to get you dressed myself?' Fabio said.

Something in his expression must have made Katie realise he meant what he was saying as without another word she turned and followed Amelia.

It was the first time Katie had flown over London, but she hardly had time to take in the sights before they were landing. She'd been given headphones to wear to drown out the noise of the engine but that had made it impossible for her and Fabio to speak. Her heart ached. Whether it was because of how Rose, Amelia and Fabio had pulled together to make this happen for her, or whether it was because she was going to say another emotional goodbye to Richard, she couldn't be sure. All she knew was that everything Fabio did made her love him more. And she didn't want to love him at all.

The helicopter touched down and Fabio helped her jump to the ground—not an easy task in three-inch heels. And then a car was pulling up and Fabio was opening the door for her.

'You'll make it. Now go.'

She looked into his familiar eyes and knew, whatever the price, she wanted this man by her side. Through good and bad. Children or no children. He had her heart and without him life had no meaning.

'Come with me.' She held out her hand. 'Be with me.' She hoped he knew what she was saying.

He hesitated for a moment as if he was going to refuse. Then he grinned and jumped in beside her. 'The invitation was for you plus one, so I guess they won't evict me.'

Inside the palace, there were more phone calls where Jonathan had to pull strings once again to get Fabio inside. However, no matter how well connected Jonathan was as Lord Cavendish, even he couldn't get an unnamed guest into the room where the Queen was bestowing the medals.

'I'll be here. Waiting,' he said. He placed his hands on either side of her face and bent his head to kiss her firmly on the lips. 'Always.'

The ceremony was as painful as Katie had expected. When Suzy stepped forward to accept the medal after the citation about Richard's heroism was read out, she had to fight tears. They weren't the only ones there that day. Too many other families were receiving posthumous medals on behalf of their dead brothers, husbands, sons, daughters, wives and sisters.

Suzy's parents were distraught, and Katie stood between them, holding their hands throughout the ceremony. When it was finally over she was relieved. She didn't know how much more she could have endured without breaking down.

Outside, as promised, Fabio was waiting. He stepped forward and introduced himself to Suzy's parents.

'My deepest sympathies on the loss of your son-in-law. You must be very proud. I hope you don't mind me intruding on this day.' He looked at Katie. 'I just wanted to check Katie was okay, but I'll leave you now.'

Suzy reached out a hand and grasped his.

'We're going to my parents' house for a bit and then back to mine. Perhaps you'll join us there later?'

'I would be delighted,' he said. 'Would it be all right if I came, Katie?'

Katie could read the hesitation in Fabio's face. 'You'd be welcome,' she said softly.

What was going on with him? His usual relaxed charm had been replaced with awkwardness. He was almost shuffling his feet.

Before she had a chance to say anything, he sketched a wave and turned back to the waiting helicopter.

Later, after Katie and Suzy's family had spent an emotional couple of hours talking about Richard, Suzy, Ricky and Katie returned home. Although there had been tears, there had been laughter too as Katie had recounted childhood escapades. Katie knew that every day she was getting closer to accepting a life without her beloved brother.

'He's some guy, your Fabio,' Suzy said.

'I don't know how many times I have to tell you, he's not my Fabio,' Katie protested.

'I'm not sure who you're trying to kid. Anyone

can see that the pair of you are crazy about each other. The way he looks at you. It's exactly the way Richard used to look at me.' Suzy's voice trembled and the two women hugged. They might be coming to terms with Richard's death but they were a long way away from being able to think of him without pain.

'I think he does love me. But he's made it clear that he doesn't want a future with me.'

'And you believe him?'

'He was pretty specific. His parents weren't exactly a glowing example of how to bring up a family, so he pretty much thinks that no relationship can survive. And that's not all.'

'Go on,' Suzy prompted.

'He can't have children. And he says no woman should be married to a man who can't give her a family.'

'Phew!' Suzy said. 'I'm not sure if that's noble or selfish.'

'What do you mean?'

'Are you sure it's not because he doesn't want to consider adoption? Or sperm donation? There are a lot of ways of getting pregnant.'

Katie thought for a moment. 'Actually, where

does he get off, deciding for me? If he loves me, he'll consider other options so we can have a family, and even if he doesn't, I'd rather have him and not have children than not have him. I don't want to be with someone because of the children they can give me.'

'Have you told him that?'

'No. I never got the chance. He's been keeping his distance. I'm not even sure that he does love me. All this could be a way of letting me down lightly.'

'Then I don't believe you know him as well as you think. C'mon, where's the Katie who would fight for what she wants? I don't know much, but I do know if you have a chance at love you have to grab it with both hands—whatever the cost.'

Katie grabbed her bag. 'You know what, Suze? You're right. If he doesn't want me, he's going to have to tell me that and I'll live with it. What I won't live with is never knowing what might have been. Now, where are my car keys?'

Fabio emerged from the shower, a towel wrapped around his waist. He couldn't put it off any longer. One way or another he had to know the results of his sperm test. He wanted Katie. Wanted her more than he'd thought it possible to want a woman. He wanted her with him every day for the rest of his life. But he wouldn't ask her to marry him as long as he knew he was infertile. He couldn't do that to her.

He picked up his mobile and studied it thoughtfully. The next few minutes could change the course of his life. Checking Dr Aubrey's number from the piece of paper, he dialled.

Katie tapped on the door, feeling nervous. All her earlier courage had evaporated. Despite her brave words to Suzy, she knew she'd be devastated if Fabio turned her down.

When he answered the door, wearing only a towel and looking as sexy as hell, it took every ounce of her resolve not to fling herself into his arms. Even if he didn't want a long-term relationship, something was better than nothing. But as soon as she thought the words, she knew she didn't believe them. She wanted Fabio, heart and soul, not just a little bit of him.

He was wearing a stunned expression on his face. No doubt he was surprised to see her here.

'Can I come in?' she said, and without waiting for a reply squeezed past him. As she did so, she caught the tantalising scent of soap.

'I was coming to see you,' he said.

'I saved you the bother.' She wasn't going to let him talk. She was going to have her say, come hell or high water.

She whirled round to face him. 'I know you love me, Fabio. I don't care what you say, I feel it in here.' She pressed a palm against her heart, knowing she was being dramatic, but she couldn't help herself. She had to make him accept that she wanted him, good or bad, madcap, reckless existence, infertility, the lot. The only part of him she would not accept, of course, was the playboy. That would definitely have to go.

'You do?' He was still looking bemused.

'Oh, yes. I may not have much experience with men but I know when someone is lying to me. You say you can't marry me, and it's something to do with not having kids and thinking that we will be like your parents and that we won't survive. I'm here to tell you that you're wrong. We will. Even if we never have children, we will be together for the rest of our lives. The chil-

dren in Brazil can become our children. And...'
She wagged her finger at him as he opened his
mouth to speak. Was that really laughter in his
dark eyes? This was so not a laughing matter.
'And,' she continued, 'we could have our own
children if we both decide that we want to. We
can adopt, we can use a sperm donor. There are
ways. But...' her voice hitched '...I don't care
about that. Not if I can't have you.'

He was looking at her in a way that made her
already rapid beating pulse beat harder.

'You would give up the chance to have children
for me?' he said wonderingly.

She nodded her head vigorously. 'I would even,
God help me, put up with you doing that big wave
surfing or whatever you call it—although don't
expect me to go and watch because I couldn't.
We don't choose the people we love, and when
we do fall in love, we shouldn't want to change
them.'

Her words dried up. She had no more to say. He
was still looking at her with an odd expression
on his face. Had she got it all completely wrong
and made a prize fool of herself? She was offer-

ing him everything she had and still he made no move towards her.

Her throat tightened and she picked up her handbag. All she wanted right now was to escape so she could lick her wounds in private.

'I just wanted you to know,' she said stiffly. 'But we can forget I said anything. I'll start looking for another job tomorrow.'

As she turned away, he grabbed her by the arm and turned her, tipping her chin and forcing her to look into his eyes.

'Say that again,' he commanded.

'Which bit? The looking for a job or the other bit?'

'The bit about loving me. Whatever.'

'I love you, Fabio. Whatever.'

He crushed her to his chest so tightly she could almost not breathe.

'And I love you. More than anything in the world. I want you with me every day of my life. I want to make you laugh, I want to make you happy and more than anything I want a little Katie to love and cherish too. And if that means IVF, so be it.'

'You will think about it?'

'More than think,' he mumbled into her hair. 'I had my sperm retested and, while the count is still so low as to be almost negligible, Dr Aubrey says that there is enough that with the help of her team and a willing, loving woman there is no reason why I can't make a baby. Maybe two or three.'

He lifted her into his arms. 'My darling Katie. Will you marry me and think about having my babies? If I promise to do everything in my power to make you happy?'

Her heart felt as if it was going to explode. She wrapped her arms around his neck and brought her mouth up to his.

'My love, haven't you been listening to a word I said?'

* * * * *

Mills & Boon® Large Print Medical

February

THE DOCTOR'S REASON TO STAY	Dianne Drake
CAREER GIRL IN THE COUNTRY	Fiona Lowe
WEDDING ON THE BABY WARD	Lucy Clark
SPECIAL CARE BABY MIRACLE	Lucy Clark
THE TORTURED REBEL	Alison Roberts
DATING DR DELICIOUS	Laura Iding

March

CORT MASON – DR DELECTABLE	Carol Marinelli
SURVIVAL GUIDE TO DATING YOUR BOSS	Fiona McArthur
RETURN OF THE MAVERICK	Sue MacKay
IT STARTED WITH A PREGNANCY	Scarlet Wilson
ITALIAN DOCTOR, NO STRINGS ATTACHED	Kate Hardy
MIRACLE TIMES TWO	Josie Metcalfe

April

BREAKING HER NO-DATES RULE	Emily Forbes
WAKING UP WITH DR OFF-LIMITS	Amy Andrews
TEMPTED BY DR DAISY	Caroline Anderson
THE FIANCÉE HE CAN'T FORGET	Caroline Anderson
A COTSWOLD CHRISTMAS BRIDE	Joanna Neil
ALL SHE WANTS FOR CHRISTMAS	Annie Claydon

Mills & Boon® Large Print Medical

May

THE CHILD WHO RESCUED CHRISTMAS	Jessica Matthews
FIREFIGHTER WITH A FROZEN HEART	Dianne Drake
MISTLETOE, MIDWIFE...MIRACLE BABY	Anne Fraser
HOW TO SAVE A MARRIAGE IN A MILLION	Leonie Knight
SWALLOWBROOK'S WINTER BRIDE	Abigail Gordon
DYNAMITE DOC OR CHRISTMAS DAD?	Marion Lennox

June

NEW DOC IN TOWN	Meredith Webber
ORPHAN UNDER THE CHRISTMAS TREE	Meredith Webber
THE NIGHT BEFORE CHRISTMAS	Alison Roberts
ONCE A GOOD GIRL...	Wendy S. Marcus
SURGEON IN A WEDDING DRESS	Sue MacKay
THE BOY WHO MADE THEM LOVE AGAIN	Scarlet Wilson

July

THE BOSS SHE CAN'T RESIST	Lucy Clark
HEART SURGEON, HERO...HUSBAND?	Susan Carlisle
DR LANGLEY: PROTECTOR OR PLAYBOY?	Joanna Neil
DAREDEVIL AND DR KATE	Leah Martyn
SPRING PROPOSAL IN SWALLOWBROOK	Abigail Gordon
DOCTOR'S GUIDE TO DATING IN THE JUNGLE	Tina Beckett